Cowboy at Heart

SHIPMENT ONE

Tex Times Ten by Tina Leonard
Runaway Cowboy by Judy Christenberry
Crazy for Lovin' You by Teresa Southwick
The Rancher Next Door by Cathy Gillen Thacker
Intimate Secrets by B.J. Daniels
Operation: Texas by Roxanne Rustand

SHIPMENT TWO

Navarro or Not by Tina Leonard
Trust a Cowboy by Judy Christenberry
Taming a Dark Horse by Stella Bagwell
The Rancher's Family Thanksgiving by Cathy Gillen Thacker
The Valentine Two-Step by RaeAnne Thayne
The Cowboy and the Bride by Marin Thomas

SHIPMENT THREE

Catching Calhoun by Tina Leonard
The Christmas Cowboy by Judy Christenberry
The Come-Back Cowboy by Jodi O'Donnell
The Rancher's Christmas Baby by Cathy Gillen Thacker
Baby Love by Victoria Pade
The Best Catch in Texas by Stella Bagwell
This Kiss by Teresa Southwick

SHIPMENT FOUR

Archer's Angels by Tina Leonard
More to Texas than Cowboys by Roz Denny Fox
The Rancher's Promise by Jodi O'Donnell
The Gentleman Rancher by Cathy Gillen Thacker
Cowboy's Baby by Victoria Pade
Having the Cowboy's Baby by Stella Bagwell

SHIPMENT FIVE

Belonging to Bandera by Tina Leonard
Court Me, Cowboy by Barbara White Daille
His Best Friend's Bride by Jodi O'Donnell
The Cowboy's Return by Linda Warren
Baby Be Mine by Victoria Pade
The Cattle Baron by Margaret Way

SHIPMENT SIX

Crockett's Seduction by Tina Leonard
Coming Home to the Cattleman by Judy Christenberry
Almost Perfect by Judy Duarte
Cowboy Dad by Cathy McDavid
Real Cowboys by Roz Denny Fox
The Rancher Wore Suits by Rita Herron
Falling for the Texas Tycoon by Karen Rose Smith

SHIPMENT SEVEN

Last's Temptation by Tina Leonard
Daddy by Choice by Marin Thomas
The Cowboy, the Baby and the Bride-to-Be by Cara Colter
Luke's Proposal by Lois Faye Dyer
The Truth About Cowboys by Margot Early
The Other Side of Paradise by Laurie Paige

SHIPMENT EIGHT

Mason's Marriage by Tina Leonard
Bride at Briar's Ridge by Margaret Way
Texas Bluff by Linda Warren
Cupid and the Cowboy by Carol Finch
The Horseman's Son by Delores Fossen
Cattleman's Bride-to-Be by Lois Faye Dyer

The rugged, masculine and independent men
of America's West know the value of hard work,
honor and family. They may be ranchers, tycoons
or the guy next door, but they're all cowboys at heart.
Don't miss any of the books in this collection!

Cowboy at Heart

THE RANCHER'S
FAMILY THANKSGIVING
CATHY GILLEN
THACKER

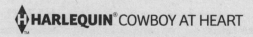

HARLEQUIN COWBOY AT HEART

Recycling programs
for this product may
not exist in your area.

ISBN-13: 978-0-373-82611-7

THE RANCHER'S FAMILY THANKSGIVING

Printed in U.S.A.

CATHY GILLEN THACKER

is married and a mother of three. She and her husband spent eighteen years in Texas and now reside in North Carolina. Her mysteries, romantic comedies and heartwarming family stories have made numerous appearances on bestseller lists, but her best reward, she says, is knowing one of her books made someone's day a little brighter. A popular Harlequin author for many years, she loves telling passionate stories with happy endings, and thinks nothing beats a good romance and a hot cup of tea! You can visit Cathy's website at www.cathygillenthacker.com for more information on her upcoming and previously published books, recipes and a list of her favorite things.

Chapter One

Expect miracles.

"Maybe it's nothing."

Susie Carrigan glared at the man she had chosen to save her from a fate worse than a hard frost on the first buds of spring.

Thirty-year-old Tyler McCabe was more than her best friend and an accomplished large animal vet. He was an astute fellow observer of human nature who could predict a person's next move with startling accuracy, a fact that made his refusal to see the gravity of her current situation all the more frustrating.

"It's not 'nothing,'" she argued.

They were in the hospital barn of Tyler's Healing Meadow Ranch, located just south of Laramie, Texas. He gave her a sexy half smile that warmed her from the inside out.

"You can't know that," he said, hunkering down to finish his task.

Susie watched Tyler stitch up the flank of a longhorn calf who'd gotten tangled up in barbed wire. As always, his touch was gentle and sure, his sutures precise.

Trying not to think how those same hands would feel on her, if the two of them ever got together again—a fact she knew darn well was as unlikely as it was secretly appealing—Susie leaned back against the stall wall. She folded her arms in front of her. "Believe me, I know this. My parents are through waiting for me and my sibs to settle down and have families of our own. The holidays will be here in a few weeks. They've got plans for me, I'm telling you."

Tyler swabbed antibiotic on the sealed wound, then covered it with a waterproof bandage. "I'd think that the heat would be off the rest of you now that Rebecca and Trevor are married."

"Precisely the problem," Susie lamented, her aggravation increasing. She looked at Tyler, studying his six-foot-four frame. Although he had an independent aura that could be a little off-putting at times—and a desire never to marry that matched her own—there wasn't a finer-looking rancher around, in her opinion. He was strong and solidly muscled, with shoulders that were broad enough to lean on. She knew, because she'd done so, every now and again. He wore his thick reddish-brown hair on the longish side, so it brushed his collar and the tops of his ears; the no-fuss style suited him perfectly. His eyes were a distinct sage green with flecks of gray, his gaze both assessing and intent. He had a habit of shaving only every couple of days. The stubble of red-brown beard that surrounded his lips only served to remind her how passionately and skillfully he could kiss. Add to that a ruggedly handsome face, a McCabe-stubborn jaw that defied anyone to try and mess with him and a smile that was reckless and intuitive enough to make her heart flutter. And best of all, when she found herself in a potentially difficult situation, he always knew what to do or say to make her feel better.

Which was, of course, why she had come to him now.

Susie scuffed the toe of her sturdy engineer's boots on the cement barn floor. "My parents think their plan to find suitable people for us to date, and hopefully marry, is what spurred Rebecca into going out and finding her perfect mate on her own. Basically, their plan worked! Now they aren't going to rest until they match up me and Amy and Jeremy, too."

"Meg and Luke can't force you to do anything you don't want to do, Suze."

Susie flushed at Tyler's use of the nickname he

had given her when they were kids. "That will not stop them from trying."

Tyler shrugged. "So tell them to back off. You'll find your own man when you're good and ready."

Susie knew what she wanted. In theory, anyway. Whoever he was, the man of her dreams wouldn't be much different from the man she saw standing in front of her.

Like Tyler, she would want her ideal someone to be taller than she was—not so easy to find for someone of her five-foot-ten-inches height—and physically fit. She'd like him to be as comfortable working with his hands as she was with hers, and to enjoy being outdoors. She'd want someone, like Tyler, who had a wealth of experience in his expression, and a twinkle of humor that cropped up in his smile at the least expected times. She'd want him to call her on her bull, and let her call him on his. To make her feel that she could tell him anything. And most importantly, she'd want him to make her feel as if everything would turn out okay.

In a perfect world, that was the man she wanted. Unfortunately, her future wasn't without potentially daunting liabilities, and in her heart of hearts, she knew it wasn't fair to any man to ask him to share in those risks. It was bad enough that she had to deal with them, without dragging anyone else into that uncertainty.

"I want you to run interference for me," Susie told Tyler.

He strode over to wash his hands in one of the sinks located at either end of the aisles between stalls. "By…"

"Going to my parents' home with me."

"No."

Susie's mouth dropped into an O of surprise. Their eyes met and held.

"I'm not going to help you put off until tomorrow what you should be taking care of today," he told her firmly.

"Thanks a bunch," Susie replied sarcastically.

Susie was used to Tyler being right there when she needed him. She wasn't used to him refusing her anything.

He shrugged and, to her increasing dissatisfaction, held his ground. "You know your parents aren't going to rest until they say whatever is on their mind. Therefore, you may as well just go on and get it done without me."

"WE CALLED YOU HERE because we're worried about you," Meg Carrigan began as she and Susie's father continued the preparations for the backyard party that would welcome Rebecca and Trevor home from their two-week honeymoon.

"It's time you moved on and forgot the past," Luke Carrigan added.

Susie tried to focus on the beauty of the November afternoon. It was unseasonably warm, with the temperature in the low seventies. The sky was a brilliant Texas blue. It made a perfect backdrop for the red, gold and orange leaves on the trees.

Susie helped her mother spread burgundy cloth on the row of tables that would hold the buffet. "That's easy for you to say. You didn't go through what I did."

Luke poured bags of ice into large galvanized tubs. "That was twelve years ago."

And it feels like yesterday, Susie thought, putting bottles of beer and soft drinks in the ice to chill. "I'm fine."

Her father moved on to setting up the barbecue grill. "If you were, you'd be dating someone."

Maybe it was because her parents were both in the medical profession, but they had always been a lot more ready to dismiss what Susie had been through than she was. "Maybe," Susie said calmly, "I'm just meant to go through life alone."

Luke frowned, taking on the gentle but commanding air of a respected physician. "And maybe you're not."

Meg smiled like the understanding nurse she

was and wrapped her arm around Susie's shoulders. "We just want you to give love a chance."

Susie tensed and stepped away. "I think they wrote a song about that."

"Susie…" Luke's voice held a warning tone.

Susie stopped rolling her eyes and sighed. "I suppose you two matchmakers have the man I should be seeing picked out, too."

"Actually," Meg allowed, "we have five."

Susie blinked. "You're kidding."

Luke set the dials on his barbecue and began layering the first of several dozen baby back ribs on the grill. "All we are asking is that you allow us to arrange for you to make their acquaintance."

"Which means," Meg added, handing her husband a platter of Fredericksburg sausages, "giving them at least thirty minutes of your undivided attention."

Susie laid out stacks of napkins, paper plates and silverware. "I can see the introductions now. Here's my daughter, Susie. She's a landscape architect who runs her own company and she can't get an evening out to save her life."

Her parents winced at her revealing choice of phrase.

"More accurately," Luke corrected, "won't accept an invitation for an evening out, from what I hear."

Susie watched her father close the top of his grill over the sizzling meat. "Why lead 'em on if my intentions aren't in the least bit serious? I'm always available for hanging out and going places with friends."

Meg sat down to shuck some corn. "It's not the same thing and you know it."

"Why is this so important to you?"

Her father now walked around the yard, setting up folding chairs. "We want to know you're moving on, especially now that the danger is over."

As far as Susie was concerned, the danger would never be over. "The heartache can still come back."

"It's unlikely." Her father came over to wrap an arm around his daughter.

"Unlikely" was not the same as "impossible," and Susie wasn't about to inflict her suffering on anyone else. "Look, Mom, Dad, I know you mean well," she said, "but I'm happy with my life the way it is." Her parents had a very happy marriage but she had a thriving business, a career she loved, a cozy house and enough money to do whatever she wanted in her leisure time.

"You could be even more content," Meg said gently.

Susie studied her parents. Luke had silver running through his sandy-blond hair. Meg covered her silver strands with an auburn rinse that matched her natural hue. Both were fit, trim and remarkably energetic for a couple in their early fifties. They could also be indefatigable when it came to getting what they wanted for their four kids. Susie propped her hands on her hips and exhaled in exasperation. "You're not going to give up on this, are you?"

Looking very much a couple, they shook their heads. "Not until you give it a try," Meg admitted.

Given the fact that Thanksgiving was only a couple weeks away, Susie was willing to do whatever necessary to keep the peace for the holidays. She lifted a hand and set her boundaries. "I'm not going husband hunting. I will agree to meet the five guys—on one condition. If it doesn't work out, if there's no chemistry or interest on either one of our parts, you two have to back off. Permanently. And swear on all that is Texas that you will never say another word about me settling down, marrying and trying to have a family ever again."

Her folks nodded, with obvious reluctance.

"How soon can we get this over with?" Susie asked impatiently.

Meg look over at the Congratulations Rebecca and Trevor! banner strung across the front porch. "I think we can arrange for you to meet all five bachelors in the next two weeks."

"WHAT'S GOING ON BETWEEN you and Susie Carrigan?" Teddy McCabe asked Tyler, several hours later. "You haven't taken your eyes off her since you arrived."

Which, unfortunately, had been late, Tyler thought. Beer in one hand, plate of barbecue in the other, he moved a little farther out in the backyard where the party was being held, and tried not to be so obvious about watching over the feistiest, most vulnerable woman he had ever known.

"Who's the guy she's been talking to?" Tyler asked.

It was clear from the range of expressions on Susie's face that the stranger was one of the guys her parents had hoped to match her up with.

"New doctor at Laramie Community Hospital. Name is Whit Jenkins. Susie's parents introduced the two of them soon after Whit arrived."

Tyler could see why Meg and Luke would hope the two would hit it off. Whit Jenkins was thirty-something, decent looking, personable. In the twenty minutes Susie had been talking to him over by the arbor, her expression had gone from pleasantly irritated—an expression Tyler knew well himself—to wary, to somewhat interested. He could tell by the way she was holding herself that she wasn't drawn to Whit in the way her parents were probably hoping, but the night was young and the man showed no sign of leaving her side, especially now that Susie's brother, Jeremy, fellow LCH physician, had joined the conversation.

"Do you know something I don't?" Teddy continued.

"Meg and Luke are fixing Susie up with five different guys in the next two weeks."

Teddy lifted a brow in surprise. "She agreed to that?"

Tyler nodded, recalling his phone conversation with Susie after the dreaded summit with her folks. She'd sounded remarkably chipper for someone who had lost the battle to keep any and all matchmaking out of her life, but Tyler wasn't fooled. Susie might go along with Meg and Luke Carrigan's wishes to keep the family peace, but she'd be privately gritting her teeth in resentment the whole time.

"So why is it bothering *you?*" Teddy asked.

Tyler looked at his brother. Teddy, Trevor and he were triplets, but the identical part only went so far as their basic looks. Teddy bred horses on his ranch, the Silverado. Trevor ran cattle on his place, the Wind Creek. Tyler's Healing Meadow Ranch was a large animal veterinary hospital.

Now the once fiercely independent Trevor was married.

The irrepressible Teddy was openly lamenting not having a wife and family.

Only Tyler knew he was not destined for the altar, now or at any time in the future.

"We both know if Susie turns to anyone, she turns to you."

"In crisis," Tyler qualified. What happened when Susie wanted more than that? Would someone like Whit Jenkins step in to claim Susie as his own? And even if Whit did, what did it matter to Tyler?

It wasn't as if he and Susie shared a romantic love. The affection they felt for each other was much deeper, and just as difficult to define. They'd never officially dated. They had tumbled into bed with each other, at last count, four times. If they both remained single, Tyler did not doubt it would happen again. And be followed, just as swiftly, by indecision and regret.

"The two of you hang out together for fun sometimes."

Tyler shrugged as he polished off the potato salad and beans on his plate. "In a group. Never alone."

"Not that hard to change—if you so desire," Teddy murmured with a probing sidelong glance.

The question was, what did he want?

Tyler put down his plate and walked back out

into the crowd to say hello to everyone he had yet to talk with at the party. He and Susie were a hell of a lot more than casual friends, yet they didn't see each other all that often. They had the ability to talk in shorthand no one else understood, and yet there were times when he didn't know what she was thinking or feeling or doing to save his life. He was always happy when he saw her. And he thought about her more than he knew he should. The two of them had cried on each other's shoulders, slept together. And stayed up all night long exchanging confidences. Yet they'd never had a single date in all the time they had known each other.

And up until now, Tyler thought, as Susie finally broke away from Whit Jenkins, that had been okay, too.

Catching Tyler's glance, Susie smiled and headed toward him.

And as usual, when he was anywhere in her radius, Tyler found he could not keep his eyes off her.

When working as a landscape architect or at the garden center she owned, she wore clothes that were ranch-hand rugged and yet sophisticated, too. Tonight, instead of the usual denim skirt or jeans, she had a soft flowing skirt of turquoise and dusty blue flowers with a ruffled hem and a silk-trimmed V-neck white knit shirt. Her small feet were encased with sturdy brown leather boots that just peeked from beneath the ruffled hem. A simple blue-and-white necklace encircled her throat, matching earrings adorned her ears.

As perfectly as the clothing draped her tall, slender frame, it was nothing compared to the captivating beauty of her face. Shoulder-length honey blond hair caught the evening light and framed her pretty face in a tumble of soft, mussed waves. Insightful amber-brown eyes gleamed beneath thin, elegant brows, the same shade as her hair. Her nose was long and straight; her high cheekbones well defined; her lips soft, pink and perfectly drawn. Her normally fair skin bore the golden hint of summer sun, and a job that had her outdoors a great deal of the time.

His pulse picked up as her favorite fragrance—a combination of flowers and citrus—engulfed him.

She linked arms with him and drew him close. Smiling up at him, she said, "I need you to come with me. Now."

"I'M GUESSING WHIT JENKINS was bachelor number one," Tyler said, as they let themselves out the back gate of the Carrigans' yard.

Susie cut across the front grass, toward the sidewalk. "Fortunately, yes."

"Why fortunately?" Tyler asked, telling himself what he felt deep in his gut was definitely not jealousy.

The edges of Susie's soft lips turned up in a triumphant smile as she waited for Tyler to catch up. "Because as it turns out Whit isn't the least bit interested in dating me. He's looking for a more dependent type of woman—someone who's more interested in staying home than running her own business."

That had been a stroke of luck. "Then why'd he agree to the meeting?" Tyler asked, unable to help but note how pretty Susie looked in the dusky evening light.

She shrugged. "He's new in town. Doesn't know anyone outside the hospital. Or he didn't, until this evening."

Tyler followed her over to her bright blue pickup truck. "You think your parents want you to hook up with a doctor?" It made sense, since Luke was a family physician and Meg a registered nurse.

"That's not why they chose Whit," Susie said with a frown. She motioned for him to get in the passenger side while she circled the front and climbed behind the wheel.

Curious, Tyler settled beside her.

"Although Whit's being a physician is part of it," Susie continued, making no effort to put her keys in the ignition. Which meant they were there to talk, not go anywhere.

Tyler shifted toward her. "I don't get it."

Susie shifted toward him. She looked Tyler straight in the eye. "Whit's an oncologist."

Tyler felt as if he'd been sucker punched. "Hedging their bets by fixing you up with a cancer specialist?" he asked quietly.

Susie's cheeks pinkened. She pleated the fabric of her long, flowing skirt between her fingers. "My guess is they thought Whit would understand what I've been through, and from that perspective, we'd have a lot in common."

Tyler tensed. "And do you?"

Susie shrugged. "I think we could be friends."

Friends sounded a lot better to Tyler than boyfriend and girlfriend. Although why he should care so much stymied him. He and Susie weren't headed for the altar. He wasn't headed for it, period. "So where are we off to?" he asked her lightly, willing to do anything to erase the hurt from her amber eyes.

"The hospital." Susie finally put the keys in the ignition, but delayed actually starting her truck's engine. "Whit asked me to look in on a patient of his. Which is why I wanted you to tag along. I don't like the idea of going in there alone."

Tyler knew Susie avoided hospitals whenever possible.

Her worst memories were set there.

"So…" Susie gave him a look he was hard-pressed to deny. "You want to follow me in your truck? Then when we're finished we can each go our separate ways?"

Tyler nodded. That was Susie, practical as ever. "I'll meet up with you in the LCH parking lot," he promised.

A few minutes later, they were walking through the entrance of Laramie Community Hospital. After a short elevator ride, they were stepping out into the hospital's brand-new oncology wing.

Susie stopped by the desk to tell the nurse she and Tyler were there to visit Emmaline Clark.

"I hope you can cheer her up. She's been pretty down," the nurse said.

An understatement, Tyler and Susie soon found out.

The pixie-faced adolescent was seated in bed, an IV hooked up to her arm. Thin and pale, she wore an auburn wig with a fake-looking sheen to it on her head. It was cut in a hairstyle for someone much older.

Her mother and father, an emotionally exhausted-looking couple in their mid-fifties, were seated in chairs adjacent to the bed. No one was talking. No one was watching the TV mounted overhead, although it was turned to a popular sitcom. There was an air of glum tension that permeated every ounce of air in the room.

Like a beam of sunshine sent down from the heavens, Susie stepped forward with a smile and extended her hand. She introduced herself and Tyler to Bill and Hedda Clark.

"You're Luke and Meg Carrigan's daughter," Hedda said.

Susie nodded. "This is Tyler McCabe, a vet at the Laramie Animal Clinic."

Tyler noted no interest at all from the patient in the bed.

"If you all want to take a break, Tyler and I can sit with Emmaline for a while," Susie offered.

The Clarks—who'd obviously been expecting Susie's visit—exchanged looks, then excused themselves politely.

"I'm not talking to anyone right now," Emmaline muttered with a pointed look at Susie the moment her parents were out of earshot. "So you may as well leave."

Susie perched on the window ledge. Despite her earlier trepidation about coming to the hospital, she looked quite calm. "Don't blame you. I never wanted to talk to anyone when I lost my hair, either."

Emmaline slowly turned her head toward Susie's empathetic tone and studied her for a moment. "You don't look sick."

"I'm not. At least I don't think I am," Susie amended quickly. "Once you've had cancer, you never know."

Emmaline turned her attention to Tyler. "Are you a survivor, too?"

He shook his head, unable to imagine what it must feel like to endure what Susie and Emmaline had.

"I brought Tyler along because he always knew what to say when I was sick." Susie patted the place next to her and Tyler sat down.

"Illness doesn't scare him," Susie continued.

Not now, anyway, Tyler thought. There had been a time...

"Yeah, well, maybe he could give my friends lessons," Emmaline said angrily. She tore off her awful wig and tossed it at the foot of the bed. It flopped to the floor. She didn't look as if she much cared what happened to it.

"I take it they've deserted you?"

"In spades. Most of them only live about an hour from here, but even before we moved, all but one or two had stopped coming by." Emmaline's lower lip trembled. Moisture glittered in her eyes. "They couldn't even be bothered to call or text message."

"The tendency when people are sick is to leave them alone so they can rest and get well," Tyler interjected gently. "Have you tried to contact them?"

Emmaline pouted. "Well...no."

"Maybe you should," Tyler said.

And maybe, Susie appeared to think, shooting Tyler a warning look only he could see, Emmaline shouldn't....

Tyler shrugged and continued anyway, "They could just be waiting to hear you're up for a visit or two or three."

"I don't know." Emmaline studied the white blanket on her bed.

"I had the same experience with my friends not coming around when I was undergoing chemotherapy," Susie said.

Emmaline lifted her head and asked Susie, "How old were you when you were diagnosed?"

"Sixteen."

Sweat beaded on the top of Emmaline's bald head. "I'm fourteen. I've been sick for two years."

"It sucks," Susie stated with heartfelt passion.

"Tell me about it." Emmaline hit the remote, and the TV clicked off. She focused all her attention on Susie. "When did you get well?"

"I had my last chemo when I was eighteen."

Her long sigh broke the silence in the room. "I hope I don't have to wait that long," Emmaline lamented.

Tyler did, too. "So what year are you in school?" he asked.

Emmaline smiled, just a little bit. "I'm a freshman, although I've yet to attend a single day of high school here. So far, all my lessons are being done at home."

A fact that only added to her loneliness, Tyler guessed. "When are you going to get to go to class again?"

Emmaline shrugged. "Maybe around the first of December if I make it through the next few weeks of chemo. Not that I know anyone here. We just moved to Laramie a couple of weeks ago."

Susie smiled sympathetically. "I'm guessing you're not liking it much so far?" she said softly.

Emmaline scowled. "The town is a lot smaller than what I'm used to. And our house doesn't have any trees or shrubs or flowers or anything, not like our last one did."

"That can be fixed," Susie said.

Emmaline ground the heel of her foot against the mattress. "My parents both work. They don't have the time to work on the yard. Probably not the money, either, since we have to pay for everything the medical insurance doesn't cover."

"So why don't you take charge of that?" Susie asked.

Emmaline looked at Susie as if she was nuts.

Tyler understood why. It did seem a ludicrous suggestion.

"What do you expect me to do from a hospital bed?" Emmaline demanded, upset.

Susie spread her hands wide. "Why, make a bargain with me, of course."

"PRETTY CLEVER OF YOU, getting the kid to agree to help you plan landscaping for the Clarks' yard," Tyler said, half an hour later. He shortened his strides to match Susie's as they walked through the half-empty hospital parking lot. It was nine o'clock, and visiting hours were ending. People were leaving in droves. "Even smarter, getting her parents to agree to let Emmaline help implement the changes, as she is physically able, and work off the cost of the plants at your landscape center."

Susie accepted Tyler's praise with a small shrug. "She can work on the design from her hospital bed. The part-time job in my center will help her meet people in the community and give her something to look forward to. And let's face it," Susie continued wistfully as the two of them stopped between their pickup trucks, parked side by side. The bright lights overhead caught the highlights in

Susie's hair and made it shimmer. "There's nothing quite as healing as being one with nature."

Tyler knew how much Susie loved being outdoors. "Except an understanding look or touch," Tyler said.

Susie nodded in agreement. A distant look came into her eyes.

"Something on your mind?" Tyler asked.

Susie ducked her head, raked her teeth across her lower lip. "It's nothing."

"Tell me."

Susie studied the painted yellow lines on the pavement, as stubborn and self-reliant as ever.

"We're not leaving here until you do," Tyler warned, knowing even if she didn't that she was beginning to need him in her life once again.

Susie dragged the round toe of her leather engineer's boot across the blacktop. "If you must know..." she conceded finally, on a reluctant sigh.

Tyler relaxed slightly. "I must."

She tucked her hands in the flowing folds of her skirt. Eventually, she lifted her head and locked eyes with him. "I'm ticked off at my parents."

No surprise there. Tyler was, too.

"For the fix-up?" Tyler guessed, wishing there were some way he could ensure that Susie would never be hurt by anything or anyone, past, present or future.

"For making this all about my cancer, once again."

And then, to Tyler's surprise, she promptly burst into tears.

Chapter Two

Sometimes the heart sees what is invisible to the eye....

Susie couldn't believe she was standing there, blubbering in the parking lot.

She could believe Tyler was right there to fold her into his big strong arms and hold her close as the emotion poured out of her in great, galvanizing waves.

It wasn't the first time she had turned to him this way. Although she was beginning to think maybe it should be the last.

It wasn't fair of her, dumping all this on him when all he had done was care about her and stand by her. The two of them were crisis-buddies, nothing more, even if they had fallen into bed together, at last count, four highly memorable times.

Even if he was the only man she had ever made love with. Or even wanted to make love with... Never mind dared get that close.

She had to get a grip. He wasn't her pillow.

Although right now with her drenching his shirt, that must be what he felt like.

She pulled away from him, wiping her eyes, and voiced the first excuse that came to mind that wouldn't lead to questions. "I'm premenstrual," she sniffed.

He chucked her beneath her chin. She should have known he wouldn't let her off easy.

"Since when?" he teased.

In an effort to shield her eyes from his probing gaze, Susie let her forehead rest against his chest. "Since…forever," she mumbled. A fresh flood of tears pressed hotly behind her eyes.

As if knowing the storm wasn't over yet, Tyler tucked her into the curve of his arm and drew her back, to lean against the passenger side of his pickup truck. "There must be something more," he murmured against the top of her head, one hand stroking down her back in long soothing strokes. "'Cause you rarely ever cry." His warm breath touched her ear. He brought her closer yet. "Not like that."

She had gotten pretty good at blinking back— or all-out hiding—discreet tears, when she was in public. It didn't mean she didn't feel incredible, overwhelming sadness sometimes.

And it didn't mean Tyler didn't pick up on the

slightest change in her mood or demeanor. If she didn't tell him now, he would just keep pestering her, keep digging, keep searching out the truth.

Finally, she shrugged.

She took the folded tissue he pressed into her hand.

Wiped her eyes. Blew her nose. And still couldn't look him in the eye. "It's everything," she said finally.

Tyler brought her back into the curve of his strong arms. His touch was more brotherly than anything else, despite their passionate past. "I'm listening," he told her in a low, gravelly voice.

Susie took another halting breath as she struggled to get her emotions under control. "If you must know, it's Rebecca and Trevor. Seeing them together tonight, just back from their honeymoon. They looked so incredibly happy together. And I'm glad for them, I really am." More than she had words to say. "But…"

Tyler nodded, even as his grip on her tightened protectively. "I felt a stab of envy, too," he admitted in a low, understanding voice.

Susie pressed on the bridge of her nose to keep more tears from falling. "Which is stupid," she continued, making no effort to hide her aggravation with herself, "because marriage has never been something I wanted."

Tyler exhaled. His big body began to relax. "Me, either."

The tears she had been doing everything to stop flowed anyway. "And yet…"

"Looking at the two of them—" Tyler picked up where she left off, as intuitive as ever where Susie was concerned "—I couldn't help but feel I was missing out on something pretty spectacular."

"Yeah." Susie forced a watery smile. She dabbed at her eyes and took in a deep breath. "Although if we see them again in a month, they'll probably be fighting over who leaves the toothpaste cap on and who leaves it off."

Tyler ruffled the hair on the top of her head playfully. He drew back, smiling now. "And even that will be spectacular."

Susie warmed at his attentiveness, even as she cautioned herself not to get used to it. Due to their busy schedules, there were times when the two of them went months without seeing each other, except for the occasional accidental meeting.

A couple other vehicles left the hospital parking lot. But Tyler seemed in no hurry to depart.

Nor was she.

She needed to talk to him tonight. She needed the special brand of comfort only he could give.

"So what else is on your mind?" he prodded.

Susie leaned against the side of the pickup truck,

the cold metal a contrast with the warmth of Tyler's tall frame. She folded her arms in front of her and looked up at the crescent moon, peeking out from behind the clouds. "I realized tonight I probably shouldn't have agreed to my mom and dad's plan to match me up with someone."

Tyler shrugged, unconcerned. He turned so he was standing with one shoulder braced against the truck, facing her. He reached over and brushed a strand of hair from her cheek and tucked it behind her ear. "So tell 'em you've changed your mind."

Susie studied the strong column of his throat, visible in the open neck of his shirt. "I made a deal. Besides—" she paused, bit her lip "—this is the only way I know to get them to back off for now."

"So you're assuming this won't work?" Tyler didn't look unhappy about that.

Nor, Susie realized, was she.

Finally, she felt herself begin to relax. And smile. "Well, duh, of course not," she said wryly. She paused to look deep into his hazel eyes, noticing all over again what a ruggedly handsome man he was. And it was more than just the symmetry of his features. It was his kindness and compassion. The humor he exhibited. The way he picked up on a person's slightest change in mood, the way he could always make a person feel better, with an offhand comment or smile.

Tyler McCabe was one man who was beautiful inside and out.

A man who revered family and friends.

A man who should not be going through life alone.

Aware he was waiting for her to continue unburdening herself, she said, "Fix-ups never work."

He squinted as if doing some inner calculations, then finally allowed in a matter-of-fact tone, "Statistically, there's probably a slight chance."

Susie blew out an exasperated breath and shifted, her knee nudging his leg slightly in the process. "Not chance enough," she muttered. The idea of living some real-life fairy tale occasionally dredged up romantic dreams she'd had about her future. But inevitably reality intervened and hit her with a terrible illness, disabusing her of any notion that she lived in a bubble, protected from all the worst things in life. Others might lead a charmed existence. Not her.

Never her.

"Some of us aren't cut out for marriage," Susie said firmly.

"I hear you."

She smiled. "So don't look for me to have an

engagement ring on my finger, because it's just not going to happen."

Was that her imagination or was that a distinctly male satisfaction gleaming in his eyes, before concern took over once again?

Tyler studied her with his usual intuitiveness. "So what else is dragging you down?"

Susie knew there was something more, too, but she couldn't figure out what.

She just knew, after she had talked to Tyler today, out at Healing Meadow, that she'd felt depressed. And her low mood had continued through the evening, only abating slightly when she had asked Tyler to go to the hospital with her.

Tyler's voice turned husky. His hand cupped her shoulder, transmitting warmth and comfort through the cloth. "Is it about Emmaline?" He paused. "Did Whit Jenkins tell you something tonight before you went to see her that you've yet to share with me?"

Susie shook her head, still holding his eyes. "It's not that. Whit told me Emmaline's prognosis was good, that they are expecting her to make a full recovery as soon as she finishes the current course of chemo. Emmaline's just depressed from the stress of treatment, and needed someone in her life who could relate. Since the hospital doesn't have a support group for teens—currently she is their only oncology patient in that age group—and she refuses to go to the regular group, he thought hoped—I would step in to be there for Emmaline."

Tyler frowned, all protective male again. "Having no idea how hard that was going to be for you."

Susie gave Tyler a look that let the handsome rancher know he did not have to go after Whit. "I've visited with adults who were sick and struggling with the disease. I've never talked to kids who were the age I was when I got diagnosed. I guess I just wasn't prepared for how swiftly it would take me back to that place."

A place she never wanted to visit again.

Suddenly aware how cold and damp the evening had become, how thin her sweater was, Susie shivered and wrapped her arms more tightly in front of her. "Or how overly emotional it would make me feel," she finished, teeth chattering slightly.

Tyler scowled, abruptly looking like a knight charged with protecting his queen. "I know you want to help Emmaline. She obviously needs comforting from someone who can relate to her. But it doesn't have to be you," Tyler instructed her firmly.

He opened the door to her truck, and guided her inside, his hand lingering on her waist until he was sure she was settled behind the wheel. "I can go see Emmaline, in your place. I can take my aunt

Kate. You know she does counseling here. She deals with stuff like this all the time."

Susie appreciated Tyler's desire to shield her from hurt, as always. This time she couldn't let him shoulder the burden. She was strong now, as capable of helping others as he was. And it was time Tyler realized that.

Susie fit her truck keys into the ignition. "Kate is wonderful. I'm sure Emmaline would appreciate seeing both of you."

Tyler rested a hand on the back of her seat and propped one boot on the running board. Elbow resting on his thigh, he studied her expression and guessed, "But you can't duck out on her."

Not and live with myself, I can't.

Susie bolstered her courage even as she turned the key. "I made a promise to her tonight, Tyler." She waited until he had closed the door for her, then put down her window and stated, just as firmly, "It's a commitment I intend to keep."

THE FOLLOWING MORNING, Tyler dropped by the Carrigans' to see Susie's parents. A Saturday, both Meg and Luke were working outside in the yard, raking leaves and weeding flower beds. As Tyler approached, he thought about how respected both were in the community. Meg was director of nursing at Laramie Community Hospital. Luke ran the family practice program that had recruited both

Tyler's cousin Riley, and their son, Jeremy Carrigan, to be on the hospital staff. They were good parents and they loved all four of their children dearly.

But they were making a mistake and it was up to Tyler to help them see it.

Hoping his meddling wouldn't be taken the wrong way, Tyler headed up the walk. The last thing he wanted to do was make Susie's life more difficult than it already was.

"Hi, Dr. Carrigan."

"Tyler." Luke put down his edger and ran a hand through his silver-blond hair.

Tyler nodded at Susie's mother. "Mrs. Carrigan."

Meg left her spade in the dirt and rose from her place beside the flower beds. Her auburn hair was mussed from the breeze stirring the fall air. Dirt and grass stained the knees of her coveralls. She smiled at Tyler, inching off her work gloves.

"Mind if I have a word with you?" Tyler asked.

"Of course not." Meg motioned him to the screened-in back porch at the rear of the large turn-of-the-century Cape Cod.

Unlike the evening before, the afternoon was pleasantly warm.

She slipped into the house and came back with three glasses of mint iced tea.

"What's up?" Luke Carrigan always got straight to the point.

Tyler sat in a cushioned wicker chair, opposite the long-married couple. "I want to talk to you about this plan to fix up Susie with four more guys."

Brows lifted. Meg and Luke exchanged the kind of husband and wife glances that brimmed with understanding but required no words. "She told you," Meg said finally.

Tyler nodded. "The first introduction didn't go so well."

"Yes, we know," Luke said.

"Whit called this morning to say he and Susie were destined to be friends. The chemistry just wasn't there." Meg made no effort to hide her disappointment.

The next was a little harder to broach. Tyler frowned. "She's upset you paired her with an oncologist."

Meg and Luke clearly did not agree with Tyler's opinion that it had been a stupid thing to do.

Giving Tyler the kind of man-to-man look that held nothing back, Luke replied, "Who better, if it had worked out?"

Me, Tyler wanted to say, though he had no idea where that thought had come from. He and Susie were not—had never been—a couple. They were crisis buddies, pure and simple.

Most of the time they were busy living their own lives. But right now Susie needed his help in the worst way.

Tyler approached her parents with the same mixture of tempered caution and compassion he used on his patients' owners.

"Susie is trying to put the disease in her past."

Meg's expression clouded with remorse. It was clear she was reacting as much as a medical professional now, as a mother.

"That's not possible, Tyler," Meg said.

Luke added, with empathy, "None of us can ever forget what Susie went through to regain her good health." He paused, looked Tyler straight in the eye, his aggravation plain. "I would think you would understand that better than anyone, given how much time you spent with Susie during her treatment."

"And every time since, when she has encountered some sort of difficulty," Meg added, with a look at her husband.

It hadn't mattered what kind of problem Susie'd had, Tyler thought. Business, personal, whatever. If she needed a shoulder to lean on, he was there. And when she no longer needed him, he just as conveniently disappeared. That way, they could maintain the status quo. It was very important to Tyler to maintain their relationship just as it was. To not do anything that would risk what he hoped would be a lifelong connection.

"And we appreciate all that you've done for her, thus far, more than we can say," Luke continued.

Not about to be cast in the role of hero now, as he had been by the Carrigans back then, Tyler shrugged. As much as he pretended Susie was just another friend, deep inside he knew that was not the case. Susie and he shared an intimacy, an ability to tell each other anything, he had with no one else, and that included his two triplet-brothers. Tyler sensed that for Susie, as close as she was to her family, she felt the same way about him. She could unburden herself to him in a way she could not confide in anyone else.

It had been that way from his very first visit to her hospital room. It was that way now, and always would be, he figured, no matter who else came and went in their lives. And if the past was any indication, other people would always come and go, since neither he nor Susie had the desire to marry and settle down.

Aware the Carrigans were waiting for him to continue explaining why he felt the need to butt into a family matter that was clearly none of his business, or should not have been, anyway, Tyler said, "I'm glad you appreciate what I've done for your daughter, but it's a two-way street. Susie has been there for me, too, when I've needed her."

Luke drained his tea. His expression shifted into Overprotective Father mode. "Unfortunately," Luke stated evenly, "we also know Susie needs a lot more in her life than you can give her as a go-to friend."

Meg held up a hand before Tyler could comment.

"Getting Susie to admit that, however, has proved difficult," Meg concurred with Luke, like a mama bear protecting her cub. "Which is why her father and I have taken matters into our own hands and given her the nudge she needs to get out there and really start living her life again. Not just day to day, the way she has been, Tyler, but with a real eye toward the future and all she has left to experience."

"I HEARD YOU STOPPED BY my folks' this morning on your way to the clinic."

Tyler looked up to see Susie framed in the doorway of his office.

He pushed back from the endless paperwork that occupied him the first and third Saturday afternoon of every month. He had hoped she wouldn't find out about his visit.

"Can't keep anything from you, can I?" he teased.

As expected, Susie refused to let his cajoling get him off the hook.

She sauntered in, looking beautiful in jeans and a white V-neck T-shirt. Four oddly shaped pearls hung pendant style around her neck from a thin piece of brown leather necklace, two more adorned her ear. Tyler smiled. Susie liked to accessorize, and her tastes ran to the unusual.

"They thought your interference was sweet but ill-advised."

Tyler noted her wavy blond hair had been drawn into a low ponytail at the nape of her neck. He knew Susie only put it back like that when the length and weight of her glossy mane was bothering her. "I take it that means there is a Bachelor Number Two on the schedule?"

She lounged next to his desk, engulfing him in her sexy flowers and citrus perfume. "Gary Hecht. A statistician. I'm meeting him for a half an hour at the driving range this evening."

With effort, Tyler shifted his gaze from the subtle curve of her hip, to her face. He tossed his pen down on his desk, rocked back in his chair. "I didn't know you golfed."

Susie made a face. "I don't. But he does." Humor glittered in her amber eyes as she acknowledged with a toss of her head, "I figured that would keep his attention focused on something other than me and make the thirty minutes go a heck of a lot quicker."

"Glad to hear you're really getting into the spirit of things," Tyler drawled.

Susie hopped up on the edge of his desk. She put her hands on either side of her, kept one foot on the floor, and swung the other leg back and forth.

"Which is where you come in," Susie said.

Tyler's hand dropped to her fingertips, curled over the edge of his desk. As always he marveled at the feminine sight. Given how much time she spent rooting around in the soil, he would have figured her hands would show the wear and tear. True, her nails were neat and short. And she almost never wore any jewelry on her hands. But her palms were every bit as silky smooth as the rest of her.

Struggling to keep his attention focused on the conversation, Tyler returned, "Oh, yeah?"

Susie nodded agreeably. Devilry colored her low tone. "I want you to accidentally on purpose show up there about the time I am supposed to leave to facilitate my exit, if things get sticky. They may not, but better safe than sorry."

The idea of rescuing her yet again was not unappealing, although Tyler pretended it was.

Watching how the autumn sunlight streaming through the open blinds brought out the honey-gold in her hair, he regarded her with mock exasperation. "And what do I get for this?"

Susie tapped the pad of her index finger against her chin in a parody of thoughtfulness. "Uh... fresh flowers for the reception desk?"

Tyler rocked back in his chair and clasped his fingers together behind his head. As far as interruptions went, this was the most pleasurable one he'd had in quite a while.

He feigned a disagreeable attitude. "You know I could care less about anything floral."

Unless it's a fragrance, adorning your skin.

Tyler didn't know why, her particular pheromones, maybe, but Susie made perfume—any perfume—smell incredible.

She squinted at him playfully and finally offered up a new bargain. "How about...hmm...I iron some of your shirts?"

His preference for unstarched cotton was a running joke between them. He fingered the pine-green oxford he was wearing. "I like 'em rumpled."

Susie swung her leg back and forth. "I'll plant a tree in front of your ranch house."

"It would just get in the way of my tractor when I mow."

Trevor wanted his off time and the chores he had to do around his Healing Meadow ranch to be as easy as possible.

"Okay, then—" she batted her eyelashes at him flirtatiously "—I'll pay for dinner."

"Now you're talking."

She held up a cautioning finger. "But it can't be here in town. It wouldn't be sensitive to ditch one date and then publicly go right out and eat a meal with another."

Tyler tried and failed to keep an amused grin off his face. "But it would be okay to do it behind Bachelor Number Two's back?"

Susie huffed and hopped off his desk. She strode back and forth restlessly. "Whose side are you on?"

As if she even had to ask. "Yours. Definitely."

"All right." Susie paused and circled her waist with her hands. She tilted her head at him thoughtfully. "So where do you want to eat?"

Tyler shrugged. "You know the area every bit as well as I do. Surprise me."

GARY HECHT TURNED OUT to be shorter than Susie by a good inch and a half, and movie-star handsome, Susie noted. He also had a great golf swing.

"I gather my parents told you I had leukemia when I was a teenager." Susie picked a spot near the end of the Armadillo Acres driving range, and set her bucket of balls down on the grass.

"Yes, they did and I immediately ran the statistics." Gary set his bucket down to the left of hers and plucked a custom club from his golf bag.

He removed the cover and ran his hand lovingly over the stem of the stick, and onto the wood head of the club, his fingers tracing the loft, as if to ensure it were still in perfect shape.

He regarded Susie with scientific enthusiasm. "Do you know that you have a greater chance of getting in a fatal car accident or contracting a deadly form of pneumonia than you do of getting cancer again?"

"No. I can't say I did," Susie said drily.

Her attempt at humor was lost on the insurance company actuary. This could be a long thirty minutes.

She loathed being stuck with a humorless companion. Being on a date with one was even worse.

Gary caught her dissatisfied look. "Illness doesn't scare me, if that's what you're worried about." Satisfied all was in order with his driver, Gary placed a golf ball on the tee and paused to line up his first shot. "And if most people looked at the numbers, I don't think it would scare them nearly as much, either. Modern medicine has done great things when it comes to improving life expectancy. Thanks to all the research being done, and new protocols developed, the odds of living a long, healthy life are getting better all the time."

Susie supposed she was living proof of that.

Now, if someone could just convince Emmaline Clark the odds were on her side, too.

"Do you talk to all your dates about this?" Susie lined up her shot, too. She swung as hard as she could. The ball went a measly twenty-five yards.

"Oh. Definitely," Gary said. A look of pure bliss crossed his features. "I love numbers."

Susie nodded. "I can see that you do." She watched Gary make a perfect line drive.

It looked as if he loved golf, too.

Gary nodded in greeting as another customer made his way past them to take up a position on the other side of Susie.

Susie started to nod, too, when she caught a whiff of man and cologne that was all too familiar. She took a good look at the cowboy ambling by, in a striped golf shirt she could swear she had never seen before, his usual denim jeans, and what looked like a pair of bowling shoes.

He kept his eyes on the green.

Gary frowned at the way Susie's mouth was

hanging open. "You know him?" Gary inclined his head at Tyler McCabe.

"I know everyone around here." Susie flashed Tyler a tight, officious smile.

This hadn't been their deal.

Tyler had been supposed to show up at seven-thirty, at the end of her "date" with Bachelor Number Two. Instead, Tyler had showed up at the beginning and positioned himself in perfect eavesdropping position.

How was she supposed to concentrate on giving Gary Hecht the attention he deserved with Tyler right beside her? It was like going on a date with her parents!

Not to mention, Tyler's golf shot was worse than hers and he kept getting his balls in her lane.

Turning her back to Tyler, Susie looked at Gary. "Tell me more about your job," she said.

Another thing Gary loved to do was talk about his life.

For the next forty minutes, she could hardly get a word in edgewise. Finally, both their buckets were empty. "Want to get more balls?" Gary asked.

"Actually, I think I'm going to have to call it an evening," Susie said. They gathered up their gear. "But there is something I'd like to talk to you about—in private." She flashed her most persuasive smile at her companion—the kind she saved for very special and or important occasions—and walked off.

TYLER COULDN'T BELIEVE IT. Susie's date had been one of the most self-absorbed men he had ever had the chance to come across, yet Susie was acting as if Gary were heaven's gift as she sauntered off with him, arm in arm.

He quickly emptied his bucket, picked up the clubs he'd borrowed from one of his cousins, and headed back to the window.

"Nice outfit, Doc." The girl behind the counter winked.

Tyler grinned. The shirt had cost him all of five bucks at the thrift shop. "You like it?"

"It's real eye-catching." The teenage clerk popped her gum. "Real, uh, orange. And green. And white. And striped." She looked down at his two-tone footwear, so different from the boots he usually wore. "I like the shoes, though." She gave the brown-and-beige leather a thumbs-up.

Funny, Tyler thought they were the ugliest things he had ever seen. They felt unsubstantial, too.

With his bagful of borrowed clubs slung over his shoulder, he headed for the parking lot. Susie was standing next to Gary Hecht's white sedan, writing what appeared to be her phone number on a piece of paper.

"Call me," he heard her say as he passed by. "And we'll set something up as soon as possible."

"Okay. I will." Gary smiled and leaned forward to brush his lips against her cheek in a standard Southern goodbye.

It was the kind of casual kiss a neighbor gave a friend. But it burned him up.

Almost as much as the sight of Susie hopping in the cab of her pickup truck and driving off without so much as a glance in his direction.

What the...

Tyler jumped in his pickup truck and drove after her. He'd expected her to laugh at his getup. Much as the teenage clerk had.

Susie had a great sense of humor and right about now Tyler felt she needed a little extra laughter in her life.

Unfortunately, his choice of clothing had apparently done little to amuse her because she did not stop until she reached the small shotgun-style house tucked away behind the landscape center she owned.

Rectangular in shape, the one-story, century-old residence was located behind three large greenhouses and the rows of trees and saplings for sale, and was hence, well separated from Carrigan Landscape Center and Design.

Her business closed at six o'clock on Saturdays. The parking lot was deserted. The two of them were very much alone, which suited Tyler just fine. He didn't want anyone else overhearing what he had to say to Susie.

Tyler got out of his truck and followed her up onto the porch.

She whirled to face him. Twin spots of pink color emphasized the elegant bones of her cheeks.

"Are you mad at me?"

Susie snorted in contempt. Lifted a brow. "Gee. You think?"

Tyler exhaled in exasperation. "Why?"

Susie set her chin. "I asked you to give me an out if I needed one." She stepped nearer. "Not chaperone the entire outing!"

Her stormy attitude added fuel to the fire of resentment burning within him. Tyler looked her up and down in a manner meant to irritate her, lingering on the curves of her breasts beneath the white T-shirt, the wide leather belt cinched around her slender waist, and the trim fit of her bootleg jeans, before returning his gaze, ever so slowly, ever so deliberately, to her flashing amber eyes. "You act like I interrupted something."

Susie's lids narrowed. She glared at him through

a fringe of thick honey blond lashes. "As it happens, you were!"

"You like that guy?" Tyler still couldn't believe she was giving the self-absorbed statistician a second chance to call her or go out with her or whatever.

"Of course I did." A fresh wave of color came into her face. "He was nice!"

"I mean as a boyfriend," Tyler clarified.

She lifted her shoulders in a stubborn little shrug. "What if I did?"

Tyler stepped nearer. "Then I'd have to say I severely misjudged you because I never envisioned you spending time with the most anal, numbers-driven guy I've ever come across in my life."

He'd never really expected her to give any guy—except him—the time of day, given the solitary way she had been living her life.

"Gary Hecht is an actuary. What did you expect?"

"I don't know," Tyler said drily. He paused to look deep into Susie's eyes. "At the very least, I figured there would have been some conversation about the great November weather."

"Well, now that would have been thrilling," Susie sassed back, mocking Tyler's sober tone.

"Certainly," Tyler continued critically, trying to impress upon Susie the need to raise her standards. "It would have been laudable if there had been a lot less talk about Gary Hecht and his interests and more focus on you."

Susie shook her head at Tyler as if she could not believe his stupidity. She stepped nearer, not stopping until they stood toe-to-toe and nose to nose. "Did it ever occur to you that I did not want Gary Hecht to focus on me?"

That had certainly been his wish, Tyler thought. It should not have been Susie's. "Exchanging information—one's likes and dislikes—is part of dating, Suze."

Susie's expression turned smug. "It wasn't dating," she informed him sweetly, batting her eyelashes Texas-belle style once again. "It was an introduction."

Tyler didn't know whether to be relieved nothing of any import had happened between Susie and Gary Hecht after all, or ticked off that Susie was goading him deliberately, trying to get a rise out of him. Or that it was working.

"Same thing, from the looks of it," Tyler muttered back.

"No," Susie countered patiently. "It wasn't." She paused a moment to let her words sink in. "I went tonight to pacify my parents. And because I wanted him to do a favor for me. Which, by the way, no thanks to you and your distracting presence, Gary readily agreed to do!"

Tyler tried not to be too thrilled that he had disrupted her powers of concentration as much as she had disrupted his this evening. "What kind of favor?" he asked.

Susie huffed, becoming difficult once again. "I'm not telling."

Tyler thought of all the ways he could force the information out of her. Kissing her, being the prime one.

"Is that so?" he countered back, his temper inching ever higher.

Amber eyes flashed. "You better believe it is."

Ignoring her sarcasm, he continued searching her face. "Don't you think you are being a little bit childish?"

She glared at him in resentment and splayed a hand across his chest. "You're one to talk! This whole discussion is absolutely stupid and juvenile and pointless and—"

Tyler had heard enough. Doing what he had wanted to do from the first moment he had laid eyes on her at the driving range this evening, he wrapped his arms around her, brought her close, lowered his head, and fastened his lips over hers. It had been an eternity since he had kissed her. Too long. All he knew was that in this moment she was everything he had ever wanted, everything he had never had. Not in any way that counted, since the two of them had made sure that every previous clinch they had shared in the last twenty-four hours had gone absolutely nowhere....

Whereas this kiss...this kiss felt as if it was going somewhere. And it was more than just the softness of her lips, or the peppermint taste of her mouth, the softness of her breasts molding against his chest, or the feel of her hands clasping the back of his neck. It was the way she was kissing him back. As if there was no tomorrow. As if there had never been a yesterday. As if this moment was all that counted, or would ever matter.

As Tyler brought Susie closer still, he knew she was right.

Tonight was all that mattered.

In so many ways, Susie was all that mattered.

Which was why he knew he had to honor their previous promise to each other and stop now, before this went any further, and the two of them ended up in bed together, again.

Calling upon every ounce of gentlemanly restraint he possessed, Tyler let the kiss come to a halt. Slowly, he lifted his head and looked into her eyes.

And even more reluctantly, let her go.

They drew apart, much more slowly than they

had ever come together. Susie had that dazed look in her eyes that was at once both deeply satisfied and yearning for more. It destroyed him every time. Tonight was no exception. He wanted her more than ever, even as he knew full well all the reasons why they should never ever be more than crisis buddies.

To do otherwise, to pretend he would always be there for her…in the way that she needed…to pretend they could ever be as emotionally close as she needed her potential soul mate to be…was pure fallacy.

Tyler knew his shortcomings.

He was not going to inflict them on Susie.

He was not ever going to put her in a position where he would hurt her, the way she had once been hurt before.

The kiss…well, the kiss had been a way to end the argument before it went too far, and either of them said or did anything they would later regret, Tyler reasoned, even as guilt washed over him, anew.

Susie stepped back, and shoved her hands through her silky blond hair.

Having recovered completely from the unexpected intimacy of the moment, she stomped her foot. "Now why did you go and do a darn fool thing like that?"

Tyler shrugged.

"Because I wanted to end the argument and that was the fastest way I knew how."

Susie's eyes took on a turbulent sheen. Her lower lip slid out into a delicious pout. "I thought we agreed…"

Tyler's gut tightened. "We wouldn't fall into bed again."

She nodded, her expression as solemn—and worried—as her mood. "It could ruin our whole crisis management system, Tyler."

A system, Tyler knew, Susie depended upon. The truth was, there had been times when Tyler really needed Susie, too. Times when she had come to his rescue.

Been there. Done what needed to be done, said what needed to be said. And then left, as soon as he was on an even keel again. Had it not been for her…

He doubted he would have survived those dark times as well as he had.

"You know I'm right," Susie persisted, her voice taking on a more normal sound.

That was the hell of it. On some level, Tyler did know.

On another…

"We set those boundaries with each other for a reason," Susie continued firmly.

Boundaries Tyler now wished—as he did every time he ended up kissing Susie—that they could take down.

"Well?" Susie prodded with a discreet lift of her brow.

A discreet lift that said she was much more relaxed about what had just happened between the two of them than he was.

She waited for his response.

Before Tyler could reply the pager at his waist went off.

He looked at the number flashing across the screen, frowned.

Susie sighed and guessed, "Emergency?"

"I hope not," Tyler groused, shoving a hand through his hair. "I don't want anything ruining our dinner plans."

He didn't want their evening ending with Susie still in a mood to regret—or was it simply dismiss—their impetuous and forbidden kiss.

Eyes locked with hers, he answered the call. Listened intently. "No problem," Tyler said when the caller had finished. "I'll be right there."

"So much for brisket, I guess," Susie lamented as he shut off the phone and put it back on his belt.

Tyler scoffed as he headed back to his truck. He reached into the compartment behind the seat, and pulled out a rumpled tan chambray shirt from the pile of clean laundry there.

He stripped off the ugly green-white-and-orange-striped golf shirt, then stood there a minute, naked from the waist up, as he put the shirt that was inside out to rights.

"I was really looking forward to treating us both to some fine Texas barbecue. Another time then, I guess."

Tyler grinned. "Are you kidding me?" Pulse racing, he shoved his arms through the sleeves of the shirt and buttoned the soft rumpled cotton cloth from the bottom up. "You're not getting off the hook that easily, missy." Now that he had her full attention, he let his gaze meet and hold hers. "You're going on this vet call with me."

Chapter Three

To get more out of life, give more of yourself.

It wasn't the first time Susie had seen Tyler without a shirt, she ruminated as she and Tyler drove to see Tyler's equine patient. She and Tyler'd been swimming together, for heaven's sake. But treading water wasn't what she thought about when she saw his broad muscular shoulders, taut pecs and strong abs.

She thought about what it would be like to be his woman. She thought about the last time they had made love. She thought about how quickly they undressed whenever they fell into each other's arms and how swiftly they put their clothes back on when reality hit them over the heads and the passion was spent. She thought about the wistful yearning she always suffered afterward. How she wished she and he had the kind of relationship where they could cuddle and share pillow talk and make love whenever they pleased, however much they pleased. She wished they could have the kind of relationship where they saw each other and hung out together all the time, even when their lives were excessively dull.

Unfortunately, that hadn't been the case in the past, and for reasons far beyond their control, would not be so in the future.

Susie exhaled in frustration.

She needed to get a grip.

Stop letting her parents' constant talk of love and romance and finding the perfect man to settle down with fill her head with romantic notions. She needed to be practical. And a realistic assessment of her recent actions indicated that she had completely overreacted to Tyler's showing up early at the driving range. True, he'd had no business hovering over her like a chaperone intent on breaking up the first sign of familiarity, but she knew he had meant well, even if he had been ridiculously overprotective.

What really annoyed her was how traitorous and guilty his mere presence had made her feel.

It wasn't as if she had been cheating on him, or was being unfaithful to him in any way. Sure, the two of them had impetuously crossed the line from friends to lovers four times in the past decade. Each time, they had promised themselves and each other there wouldn't be a next time.

Each time, there had been a very good reason.

The first time they had come together like that had been on her twenty-first birthday. She was feeling sorry for herself, thinking that because of her illness, and the possibility it may come back, she would never get close enough to anyone to make love. Tyler had told her she was wrong, and the next thing they knew they had ended up in her dorm room bed. She had pushed him away afterward, accepting that it never should have happened.

The second time had been four years later, when he had passed his boards and gotten his license to practice veterinary medicine. He'd called her, wanting to celebrate. They'd had way too many margaritas. And somehow ended up in bed, again. That time they'd fallen asleep afterward. They'd awakened at dawn, hung over, happy—about his success—but mortified by their lapse in judgment.

It had been awkward for them for a while. They were both embarrassed by the sheer physical abandon with which they'd given themselves to each other. But eventually they'd chalked it up to an alcoholic and joyful aberration and gone back to being crisis buddies once again.

Which of course was how the third time had come about, several years after that.

One of Tyler's college friends had been killed in

an accident, and he'd been devastated by his buddy's death. Susie had gone to the funeral in Corpus Christi with Tyler and they'd ended up talking in their hotel room late into the night. Tyler had been so sad, so devastated, it had seemed only right that Susie reach out to him. One hug had turned into two. Before she had known it, they were kissing again, and once they started kissing, there was no reason either of them could think of to stop. Fueled by grief and sadness and the need to feel, in that instant, very much alive, they had tumbled right back into bed.

They'd made love through the night that time. Fiercely, passionately.

By the time morning came, they had come to grips with the passing of his friend. But were more confused than ever about what had transpired between them. They knew it wouldn't have happened had the two of them been back in Laramie, Tyler not reeling with grief. So again, they had promised themselves. No more.

And that vow had held until the day a year before, when Susie'd had a close call on the job. She was out doing a bid on a property, inspecting a tree that had died and needed to be removed, when one of the rotting limbs broke off and came down, knocking her to the ground, narrowly missing her head. Her crew had insisted she go to the hospital and get checked out. Her parents had overreacted even though all Susie had to show for the near-death experience was a few bruises and a torn shirt.

Meg and Luke had wanted her to go home with them.

She'd called Tyler and had him come and get her instead.

Tyler had told her parents he would stay with Susie through the night—a move that had turned out to be both good and bad. Good because when the enormity of what had nearly happened finally hit Susie she had started crying and couldn't stop. Tyler had held her until the storm passed, and a different storm started. Once again, they had ended up in her bed.

Making love with him that night had been the perfect remedy for the calamity. The usual confusion and promises not to ever do it again had followed. And they had kept that promise. Until tonight.

The fact they had ended up in each other's arms this evening really was no surprise, Susie silently reassured herself.

Her parents had a talent for driving her absolutely crazy. And now, thanks to her plea for his intervention, Tyler was being driven to distraction by the situation, too.

Fortunately, this time, for the first time, their coming together like that had started and ended with a single kiss. His emergency call had removed them from a situation rife with physical temptation and emotional pitfalls.

And now that she had gotten the much-needed break, she had to take a step back. Take a deep breath, and go back to what worked best for her, living moment to moment. No plans for the future, other than the ones she had for her business.

The upcoming holidays were going to be tough enough without adding another emotionally complicated but ultimately going-nowhere lovemaking session with Tyler to the mix. Thanksgiving was so family-centered. It always brought home to her the things that would never be hers—a husband, children, the deep, inherent belief she would have everything she had ever wanted, everything she deserved, and live to a ripe old age.

All that and more had been taken from her. She didn't care what anyone said. No platitude or encouragement could bring it back.

"Still ticked off at me for kissing you that way?" Tyler drawled, turning his pickup into the fair grounds where the Laramie County barrel racing competition was being held.

How could she be mad at him when she was equally to blame?

Susie flashed a smile. "Not a problem as long as you don't do it again."

Tyler's expression remained inscrutable. He searched for a parking place. "I'll keep that in mind."

Which was not the same thing as promising to abstain, Susie noted.

Jimmy Rooney and his father met them at the entrance to the horse barn. Mr. Rooney was a mild-looking man, unlike his son, who seemed like an arrogant kid.

Susie sized up the sixteen-year-old with the custom-made Western clothing, expensive hat and hand-tooled boots, and the fifty-year-old man beside him. She figured out two things right off the bat. The kid was in charge here, not the parent, and the kid was trouble.

Mr. Rooney shook hands with Tyler. Unlike his son, he was all grace and warmth. "I'd like you to examine Catastrophe. I thought he was favoring his right front leg during the warm-up, but couldn't be sure."

"I told you, Dad. I didn't feel anything out of the ordinary when I was riding him!" Jimmy Rooney glared at Tyler. "You'll see. Nothing is wrong with my horse. Nothing that would keep me from racing him tonight anyway." Jimmy brushed past the other contestants in the barn, and led the way to the stall where his horse was quartered.

With a gentle word to the sleek stallion, Tyler entered the stall and squatted to examine the dark brown quarter horse, with the glossy black mane and tail. "I can feel the heat in this leg."

Jimmy sent a panicked, angry look at his father. "We're supposed to compete tonight!" Jimmy turned to Tyler with a haughty glare. "It's for the area championship."

Tyler examined the rest of the horse, then settled next to the right front leg once again. As Tyler pressed gently, the horse snorted in response and attempted to push Tyler's hand away by rubbing his head against his right leg.

Tyler petted Castastrophe, then stood and spoke gently in his ear. The horse calmed under Tyler's ministering touch.

Tyler turned to Jimmy and his father. "I know this is disappointing, but I advise against racing Catastrophe tonight. His leg needs to be wrapped and iced."

Jimmy erupted in resentment. "We can do that after!"

Tyler stated firmly and deliberately, "You both understand, if you race Catastrophe like this, you risk permanent injury to the leg."

Jimmy looked at his father for help.

Mr. Rooney folded like an accordion fan. Arms aloft, he tried to play peacemaker between son and vet. "It's just one race, Doc, and the winner gets to go on to an even bigger competition next week."

Tyler shook his head, his expression grim. "Sorry, I can't sanction it."

Jimmy stepped between his father and Tyler. "He's just trying to scare us, Dad. I mean, look at Catastrophe. He's still putting weight on that leg. You can't even see any swelling. I'm sure he'll be fine for tonight's race. And we'll ice and wrap it after."

It was obvious Mr. Rooney was putting more value on what his son wanted than on what was best for the beautiful stallion. The decision had been made, and it wasn't in the best interest of the quarter horse. "You can stay and check Catastrophe after the event, can't you?"

Tyler paused. Susie knew he was tempted to walk away, not wanting any part in the bad decision.

And yet, should something bad happen, Tyler definitely wanted to be here to offer whatever veterinary assistance was required.

"I'll stay through the race," Tyler muttered unhappily.

"How can you stand having your veterinary advice ignored like that?" Susie asked as she and

Tyler left the horse barn and made their way to the bleachers.

Tyler sat down and watched the women's barrel race. The riders came out of the gate at full speed, and tore around the randomly placed barrels as quickly as possible.

It was an exciting event, but, Susie could see, tough on the animals making the breakneck turns at top speed. It was no wonder Tyler was concerned about the fate of the quarter horse in his veterinary care. The lack of regard on the Rooneys' part was sickening.

"It bites," Tyler admitted, over the blare of the fairground's loudspeaker. He waited until the last contestant's time was announced, before turning to her and continuing, "But it's part of the job."

So Tyler accepted it, just as he had always advised her to do.

Susie watched another horse and rider come out of the gate. She turned back to Tyler. "You think Catastrophe will be okay?"

Tyler grimaced. The worried look was back in his hazel eyes. And this time he made no attempt to hide it.

"I hope so," he said.

"I TOLD YOU HE'D BE all right," Jimmy Rooney said afterward, holding his first place trophy.

Ignoring the goading triumph in the boy's tone,

Tyler wrapped Catastrophe's leg and packed it in ice. As Susie watched, she could not help but be impressed by Tyler's skill.

"It's very important you rest your horse until all the swelling and tenderness is gone," he said. "That will probably take two to three weeks." Tyler reassuringly patted the horse's side. "And I'd like to see him and give the okay before you race him again."

"But the state competition is next week!" Jimmy exclaimed.

Tyler looked at Mr. Rooney but didn't bother to repeat his earlier advice. "If there are any changes, you let me know. In the meantime," Tyler said as he wrote out a list, "be sure you follow these instructions."

Jimmy glared at Tyler and stalked off, trophy still in hand.

"Thanks for coming out, Doc." Mr. Rooney took the list of instructions and shook Tyler's hand.

Tyler nodded his acceptance. He paused to run a gentle hand down Catastrophe's face, then turned and walked with Susie out of the barn.

Susie's steps meshed with Tyler's as they threaded their way through the parking lot. "You're still worried."

Tyler went around a pickup and horse trailer. "Yep."

"Nothing else you can do?" Susie was so busy looking at Tyler she didn't see the pothole in front of her.

"Nope." Tyler caught her arm before she fell. He steadied her a moment before he released her. "Catastrophe's not my horse, unfortunately."

Trying not to think how nice that brief touch had been, Susie consulted her watch. "About the dinner I owe you. The place I was going to take you tonight is closed."

Tyler shrugged. "What is open?"

"For dinner?" In the city, they would've had no problem. But Laramie County was a different story.... "Everything in town stops serving by eleven."

"Which means by the time we get there, we're going to be out of luck." Tyler exhaled.

Knowing it was her turn to cheer him up, Susie drawled, "Not necessarily." When he looked at her, she winked, "Meet me at the truck."

Already smiling, he winked back. "Will do."

Susie hurried away and returned minutes later, her arms packed. "The concession stand still had a few items left. Want to eat in the cab or in the back?"

"It's a nice night." Tyler lowered the tailgate on his pickup truck. He took the horse blanket he carried in his toolbox out and spread it over the bed of the truck. Susie set their feast down, then allowed him to help her up into the back. They sat cross-legged in the moonlight, while all around them what few people remained loaded their horses into trailers and drove off.

"So what do we have here?" Tyler asked.

Susie began unloading the cardboard containers. "Two Frito pies—"

"Ah." Tyler grinned as he took the lid off the steaming concoction. "Spicy Texas chili, cheese, onion and corn chips. Who can resist that?"

Susie grinned. "Not either one of us, that's for sure. Plus I got an order of French fries. A couple of corn dogs, and funnel cakes for dessert. One lemonade, one root beer, and two large dill pickles."

Tyler chuckled. They spread out their bounty and dug in. "You know what this reminds me of?"

There'd only been one other time they had eaten in the back of his pickup truck. "The year I was sixteen," she said.

Tyler put a straw in his lemonade. "And so pissed off because you were sick."

Susie made a face. "I was pissed off because my parents wouldn't let me do anything or go anywhere because flu season had started and they were afraid I'd get it."

He lifted a dissenting brow. "A valid concern,

since your immune system was temporarily damaged by the chemotherapy."

Susie savored the spicy food. "But I didn't care," she said with a wave of her plastic spoon.

Tyler stretched his leg out straight, so it was next to hers. "You just wanted your freedom back."

Susie rested her back against the metal sides of the truck bed and uncurled her legs, too. "And you took pity on me and helped me sneak out of the house after curfew."

Tyler shook his head in silent remonstration. "We were darn lucky we didn't get busted."

"Amy knew."

Tyler gave her a look that had her pulse jumping.

Aware it wasn't as much a betrayal as it sounded, Susie shrugged. "Well, I had to have somebody there to run interference for me if need be. And I knew she'd think it was all romantic." As soon as the words were out, Susie flushed.

Tyler's expression softened. The last of the other pickups was leaving the lot. "Amy needn't have worried. I couldn't put the moves on you back then. You were way too fragile."

Susie chuckled and dipped a fry in ketchup. "Yeah. The moves came later."

He pretended affront. "I've never put the moves on you."

Susie figured they might as well talk about it, she'd been thinking about it so much. "We've made love four times, Tyler," she reminded softly.

An inscrutable expression crossed his handsome face. He shifted restlessly. "Yeah, but that was different."

"True." Susie exhaled sadly, thinking back, wishing and wanting. "Our coming together wasn't so much all-out lust as the need to comfort and be comforted."

"Fortunately," Tyler reached across to pat her knee familiarly, "things are better for us now."

"You're right," Susie conceded, albeit somewhat reluctantly. Why, she couldn't think. "There is no real crisis. Or there won't be once I meet the other three bachelors and get through the Thanksgiving holiday," Susie amended hastily, wondering why the notion of not needing Tyler to run interference for her once again left her feeling so bereft.

Deciding the upcoming holidays had left her feeling uncharacteristically sentimental, and that the emotion would fade when January and the New Year rolled around, she looked into his eyes. "Speaking of which, did you get a message on your answering machine today about a McCabe-Lockhart-Carrigan-Chamberlain-Remington-Anderson family preevent-planning meeting tomorrow afternoon?"

"We don't have to go." Tyler helped her pack up the remnants of their meal. "If we don't show up, they'll just assign us something to do."

The less holiday preparations she had to endure, the better, Susie decided. She allowed Tyler to give her a hand down, the same way he'd given her a hand up. "Sounds good to me," she said.

"So what was your holiday assignment?" Tyler asked Susie early the next evening, when they ran into each other in the hospital parking lot.

She looked really pretty in a burnt-red sweater with an open neck, long, silky paisley skirt, and fancy cowgirl boots. She'd drawn her hair back into a knot at the nape of her neck. A red, white, green and brown beaded necklace with a sterling silver heart at the center of it adorned her neck. Silver drops dangled from her ears. He could smell her citrus and floral perfume.

He knew he was looking at her like a kick-ass woman instead of a "friend."

Not that she seemed to notice or view him in the same way. No, she was looking at him, same as always, with gentle eyes and a wry, self-effacing smile.

Susie shut the driver side door and walked around to the passenger side. "I have to make gratitude books, filled with inspirational quotes but leaving room for the recipients own 'thank-

ful for' list for all two hundred and fifty guests."
Susie's teeth sank into her plump lower lip. "Can
you believe that?"

Tyler stepped back so she could open the passenger door. "It sounds like a good idea."

Susie made a face. "It's also no coincidence the
task was assigned to me," she said with resentment.

Tyler tore his eyes from her slender backside as
she leaned into the cab, and lifted a canvas carryall
from behind the seat. "Back to the Big *C* again."

"Right." Susie dumped a stack of landscaping
books onto the passenger seat. "Everybody just
naturally figures because I've had cancer that I
know how precious life is."

Tyler watched her sort through the titles. "Don't
you?"

"Well, yes," Susie allowed, turning and handing him a hefty volume, "but that's not the point."

Figuring this was going to take a while, Tyler
settled in beside her. "The point is you don't want
to be singled out as some great survivor."

"Right." Susie put two books back in the carryall and handed him a slim tome. "I just want
to be normal. If that's even possible." She shook
her head and looked at the dark sky overhead,
which seemed remarkably devoid of stars for a
clear Texas night. "I'm not sure it is."

Tyler wondered if Susie knew how pretty she was. Inside and out. Probably not, judging by her cantankerous expression. "It probably would be possible for you to feel 'normal'—whatever the heck that is—if you got married and settled down like they want."

Susie whirled in a drift of perfume. She propped her hands on her hips and glared at him. "You really don't want to go there, Tyler."

"I don't know," Tyler drawled, deciding to try and tease her into a better mood. He flashed a provoking smile. Shifting the books to one arm, he reached out and touched her cheek. "I kind of like the fire in your eyes when you get irked."

Susie made another face at him and let that one pass, he figured, only because she feared if she pursued it the two of them might end up doing something foolish again, like kiss. It was a good instinct on her part. Tyler couldn't say why. He just knew he'd been thinking about her nonstop all day. Wanting to kiss her again, too.

And how foolhardy was that?

"What was your Thanksgiving assignment?" Susie asked.

Now it was his turn to need cheering up....

Tyler admitted, "Something equally painful to me. I have to make apple, pumpkin and pecan pies."

Susie's eyes widened. "They know you can't cook!"

"Yeah, well," Tyler grumbled, "I think that was the point. All the moms know I'm going to have to go to some female for help."

Susie studied him. "Got anyone in mind?"

Tyler beamed. When opportunity knocked... "Glad you asked. As a matter of fact, I do."

Knowing where this was heading, she held up a hand. "No…"

"You're a fabulous cook."

"Only because I had nothing else to do those months I was sick and my mom let me amuse myself by giving me free rein in the kitchen."

"And that time certainly paid off." He rubbed the pad of his thumb across her chin. "So how about it? Will you help me make some pies?"

Susie looked deep into his eyes. "On one condition."

Tyler dropped his hand and snapped his fingers. "I knew it," he lamented dramatically. "There's always a condition with you."

She stuck out her tongue at him, and continued firmly, "You have to help me find the quotes and design the stupid gratitude books."

Spending time alone with Susie was not exactly what he would call a hardship, even if they were doing a task she would prefer not to be executing. "If I do it, it's not going to be stupid," Tyler warned.

Susie scoffed and added two more slim landscaping plant volumes to the ones he was already holding. "Please. You're one of the least sentimental guys I know."

Tyler pressed his free hand over his heart. "I'm wounded."

She didn't buy it. "You wish."

He turned serious. "I'll help you."

"Thank you." Susie shut the door and locked her truck.

"Where are we going with these books, by the way?"

"Up to see Emmaline. I want her to make a list of all the flowers and trees that she likes. She's got a chemo treatment tomorrow that's going to run for half the day. It'll give her something to do while she's getting the IV."

"Good thinking."

Susie edged closer to Tyler. "I really feel for her."

"I know you do." Tyler gave Susie's shoulders a companionable squeeze. "I do, too."

Briefly, she turned her head and rested her face against his shoulder. "Life just isn't fair sometimes."

"You're right. It isn't." Tyler paused to wait their

turn at the lobby door. He used the opportunity to lose himself in her eyes. "But we have to soldier on nonetheless."

Susie's expression went from wistful to cynical in sixty seconds. Too late, Tyler realized that was exactly the kind of platitude she would have expected from a guy.

"I think I have my first quote for the gratitude book," she said drily, as the two of them crossed the lobby and stepped into the elevator.

Tyler accepted Susie's ribbing in the good-natured way it was given. He remembered how much his "when-the-going-gets-tough, the-tough-get-going" attitude had helped her when she was sick, even if it sometimes made her mad as hell. The same advice had helped him innumerable times.

Tyler pretended pique even though he knew his eyes were as alight with amusement as hers. "Good as my advice is, I think the event planners had something much more eloquent—"

"Don't you mean touchy-feely?"

"—in mind for the journal," he finished. "And you—"

"Make that we," Susie corrected.

"—better deliver," Tyler said seriously, "or our mothers are going to send us right back to the drawing board."

"HI, EMMALINE." SUSIE AND TYLER entered her hospital room together.

Emmaline held up a hand and continued writing.

"Have we come at a bad time?" Susie asked.

"No. It's okay." Emmaline finished and put down her pen. Her pale face radiated with happiness. "I'm just addressing envelopes. My parents said I could invite all my old girlfriends over for a slumber party the weekend before Thanksgiving."

"That sounds like a great idea," Tyler said.

Emmaline blushed and fiddled with the knit cap on her head. "Thanks for making me realize that my friends weren't psychic. I guess I haven't been very good at keeping in touch with them, either. Hopefully, a party at my house will help us feel close again." Emmaline looked at the books Tyler was carrying. "What have you-all got there?"

"Something important for you to study." Susie sat down beside Emmaline. Tyler handed over the books and hung out with them while they selected all the shrubs, trees and flowers that appealed to Emmaline. When they had finished, Susie encouraged Emmaline to show what she liked to her parents and get their input, too.

"Call me when you've made your choices and I'll set up a time to take a look at your yard, so we can plan the next phase of the landscaping," Susie said.

"I will. And thanks, Susie," Emmaline said.

"No problem." Susie grinned.

"You, too, Tyler." Emmaline beamed. "It was nice of you to stop by to see me."

Tyler gave the ailing teenager a high five. "Good luck with your treatment tomorrow."

Susie echoed the sentiment. She and Tyler headed out.

"What's worrying you?" Tyler asked the moment they were alone.

Susie shrugged. She should have known she couldn't hide anything from Tyler. "I hope that slumber party isn't a mistake."

Tyler frowned. The two of them stepped onto the elevator. "Why do you think it would be?"

Susie drew a deep, bolstering breath. "Because her friends might not all come."

Tyler remained puzzled. "If even a few do, I'm sure she'll be happy."

Susie rubbed at the bridge of her nose. "You don't know what it's like, to have to reach out to people you thought were your friends, and be turned away."

"So what's the alternative? Should we be encouraging her to stay isolated?"

Aware he'd struck a nerve, Susie turned her

glance toward the lights above the steel doors. "There have to be kids here in Laramie who would be willing to be her friend."

"It's not the same as choosing your own friends."

"Right." Susie stepped out into the lobby. She waved at the volunteer at the information desk. "Anyone who would make friends with Emmaline now would sign up knowing she's had a tough time of it, and could have an even tougher time ahead." Susie stopped and turned so abruptly she ran into Tyler's chest. "You didn't desert me."

He steadied her with a hand to her elbow, stepped back slightly. "That's because I'm special." His voice was a low, sexy rumble.

The edges of Susie's lips curled in aggravation. "You know what I mean," she chided.

Compassion shone in his hazel eyes. "I know you worry too much sometimes."

An intimate silence fell between them.

Abruptly, Susie had the feeling that Tyler wanted to kiss her again but wouldn't—for reasons that had nothing to do with the fact they were standing in the hospital lobby, where everyone and anyone could see.

With effort, she pulled herself together. "So." Susie swallowed around the parched feeling of her throat. "When are you going to help me find all those stupid platitudes to put in our gratitude journals?"

Looking relieved the testy banter between them had picked up once again, Tyler censured her with a look of exaggerated impatience. "Good attitude. And for your information, missy—" he tapped her playfully on the cheek "—nothing I offer up will be 'stupid.'"

"Hokey, then," Susie corrected, teasing him right back. "And that," she goaded him with a playful tap on the center of his chest, "remains to be seen." She bet he could do hokey as well as the next person, if so moved.

Tyler looked deep into her eyes as she slowly dropped her hand to her side once again. "Cynical to the core, aren't you?"

"Mmm-hmm," Susie admitted happily. She propped her hands on her slender hips. "So where are we going to look for this stuff?"

Tyler shrugged his broad shoulders affably. "The internet?"

THEY ENDED UP AT SUSIE'S house because she had a DSL line. He couldn't get one out at his ranch. So it was either her place or the vet clinic, and her place was definitely cozier.

For as long as Tyler could recall, Susie had been into comfort. That was reflected in the overstuffed red twill sofa and matching club chairs in the living room at the very front of her home, the curved leather banquette in the kitchen, and the big old-fashioned sleigh bed in her bedroom.

Like other "shotgun houses" of the early 1900s, the abode was one room wide, with a living room in front, an eat-in kitchen and laundry directly behind that, bedroom and bath at the very rear of the dwelling.

Susie had updated the interior with wide plank wood floors, soothing cappuccino walls that allowed her to change the color scheme as often as she wanted—which turned out to be a couple of times a year—and a mix of funky posters, stunningly serene oil paintings and of course, lots of leafy green houseplants and flowers.

"This is a lot harder than I thought it was going to be," Susie mused, staring at her laptop.

Tyler went to her refrigerator, helped himself to a root beer and brought one for her.

Truth was, he didn't care how long this took. He could happily spend days whiling away the time with her. "That's probably because we're going about it in the wrong way." He twisted off the cap before handing her the bottle.

Susie tore her gaze from the computer screen. The fire of indignation lit up her amber eyes. "Okay, smarty-pants, tell me how we should be going about it."

Trying not to think how pretty she looked with her flushed cheeks and slightly mussed hair, Tyler took a swig of root beer. "Forget the computer. Let's do this off the top of our heads."

Susie reached up to take the pins out of her hair. "I'm not sure either of us is that gushy."

Tyler watched the wavy blond mass fall loose and free to her shoulders once again. "We don't have to be gushy."

Susie removed her earrings, one after another. Then her necklace. She put all on the coffee table, next to her boot-clad feet. "Tell that to our mothers. I dare you."

Able to see where this was going—when her jewelry went, her shoes did, too—Tyler leaned forward to help her off with her cowgirl boots. "The point of the gratitude journals," he said, as he removed them, one at a time, "is just to give a jumping-off point for people's own thoughts and feelings, a retrospective of the year, right?"

"Yes." Susie smiled her thanks as she wiggled her toes inside her socks, then rubbed them, one against the other. Sighing, she stretched her legs, which were still covered nearly to the ankle by the silky fabric of her paisley skirt. "There's supposed to be some type of platitude or familiar truism at the top of each page that has something to do with

Thanksgiving, and that's what is stumping me," Susie continued.

Tyler settled beside her, close enough so he could see the computer screen, too.

Susie released a troubled sigh as she lifted her arms and ran her fingers through her hair. She kept her hands clasped behind her neck. "When I think of the holiday all I'm coming up with are symbols like Pilgrims and Indians and a great meal and too much football and way too many dishes…."

With Herculean effort, Tyler did his best to keep his eyes on Susie's face.

She was obviously unaware of the way her current posture was showcasing the lusciousness of her breasts.

That did not, unfortunately, mean he was unaware.

He could feel himself getting hard.

Not good.

Not good at all.

Tyler gritted his teeth and did his best to think of all things frigid. Polar ice caps. Showers in the dead of winter when the water heater was on the fritz. Snowballs dumped down the back of your neck…

"And as we've just demonstrated, the internet

is proving of no help," Susie continued in mounting frustration.

Tyler closed his eyes so he could concentrate on what she was saying. Not the sexual frustration he was suddenly feeling.

"That's because the internet doesn't know what's in your heart." Tyler opened his eyes and nodded at the center of her chest. Too late, he realized that was a bad idea. "Or mine or anyone else's," he added quickly, shifting his posture slightly to ease the building pressure at the front of his jeans.

Susie abruptly dropped her arms, straightened her spine and let her feet fall back on the floor. "I'm not sure I know what's in there," Susie muttered, obviously talking about her heart.

Tyler stared at the screen again, then stood. It would be best if he put some physical distance between the two of them for a minute or two. "Let's try another approach." He rubbed his hand across his forehead. Looked out her front window. Examined some green leafy plants, at length. "Let's make a list of familiar sayings that have meant something to us in our lives. Stuff we hear all the time, and apply in one way or another to what we are doing and thinking." Sure he had himself under control, he turned back to her.

She was grinning now, as if greatly amused.

"Like 'don't squat with your spurs on' and 'don't dig for water under the outhouse'?" she guessed.

"Not to mention 'never ask a man the size of his spread,'" Tyler quipped.

They both chuckled.

"But I doubt our mothers and aunts would appreciate those sentiments showing up in the Thanksgiving journals, even if the men would," he said.

Susie exhaled in obvious disappointment. "So curtail the Texas-isms."

"For the most part, yeah."

"So what are some of your favorite mottos?" Susie asked.

Tyler had to think a moment. "The simple ones, I guess, like 'be true to yourself.' And 'count your blessings.'"

"I've got one on the wall of my office. It says 'if you do enough small things right, big things can happen.'"

"See? We've got the knowledge right here." Tyler pointed to her head, and his. "All we have to do is access it."

Susie started typing. "Okay, cowboy," she told him brightly, "give me all you've got."

For the next two hours, they came up with slogan after slogan.

"Now all we have to do is narrow them down

to the twenty or so they asked me to put in the gratitude books."

Wondering why the two of them didn't just hang out together more often, Tyler shrugged, adding, "It shouldn't be too hard, although you may want to think about it for a few days. It's possible we could come up with a few more."

Susie nodded just as the pager on Tyler's belt went off.

He frowned. It was part of his job to be on call, even on the weekends. He hated having his time with Susie interrupted. "Sorry."

She waved off the untoward interruption. "It's okay."

Tyler lifted the phone to his ear. "Doc McCabe here. Hello, Mr. Rooney. Oh. All right, don't do anything. I'll be right there."

Susie looked as concerned as Tyler felt. "What's up?"

Keys in hand, Tyler was already heading for the door. "It's Catastrophe. He's in trouble."

Chapter Four

For everything there is a season.

Catastrophe lay in the corral at the Rooney ranch, whinnying softly, eyes glazed with pain. Tyler set his vet bag down in the dirt and bent over the magnificent animal. It didn't take long for his worst fears to be confirmed.

"The leg is broken all right." Tyler stroked the quarter horse gently, then reached into his bag and pulled out a syringe and a glass bottle.

A glance at Susie—who had insisted upon accompanying him, as soon as she had heard where Tyler was going—showed she was every bit as upset as he was by the disregard for the beautiful, spirited animal's welfare.

Tyler stared down the kid who was responsible. "What were you doing barrel racing him tonight?"

Jimmy Rooney paced back and forth while Tyler administered the medication.

Tyler noted the kid looked more put-out than

sorry about the disaster his selfishness had brought about.

"I had to practice for next week's event," Jimmy declared stubbornly.

Catching sight of the ire on both Susie's and Tyler's faces, the kid whined, "I let him rest all day."

Tyler brought out a splint and moved down to immobilize the leg. "One day wasn't enough. He needed several weeks. I told you that."

Mr. Rooney stepped forward. Clearly distraught and feeling the guilt and compassion his son evidently did not, he watched as Tyler secured the splint. He ran a hand over his eyes. "Look, there's no use arguing over what's already happened," Mr. Rooney told Tyler miserably.

Jimmy pushed forward. "Is Catastrophe going to be able to race again?"

Tyler ran a hand over Catastrophe's belly, glad the horse's agonizing whinnying had subsided. Tyler sat back on his haunches, trying to think about the best way to proceed. "No."

"Then put him down," Jimmy snarled.

Mr. Rooney turned to his son.

"Catastrophe's no use to me now," Jimmy declared.

Tyler got to his feet and faced Mr. Rooney. "Let's not be hasty. You can still offer Catastrophe for stud service."

"We'd have to get him well first." Mr. Rooney frowned.

"Who cares about that?" Jimmy fumed. "I need a new horse to ride by next week!"

Sweat broke out on Mr. Rooney's face. "How much is it going to cost to fix that leg?"

Tyler named the fee, which stretched into the thousands.

Mr. Rooney paled.

"See what I mean, Dad?" Jimmy Rooney argued. "It would be cheaper and easier to get a new horse."

Tyler curbed his temper with effort. It wasn't easy. He wanted to deck the kid, and shake some sense into the wimpy dad, who had—by his own weakness—let his child turn into such a selfish, unfeeling monster. "Then I'll take Catastrophe," Tyler said flatly, refusing to destroy an animal for nothing more than the convenience of the neglectful owners. "I'll waive my fees, including my visit to the fairgrounds last night, in exchange for the animal."

Mr. Rooney looked relieved. He glanced at his son.

Jimmy threw up his arms in disgust. "I told you," he nearly shouted. "I don't care what you do with this worthless stallion. Just get him out of here!"

Mr. Rooney turned back to Tyler. "If that's what you want to do, then yes, we agree. How soon can you move him?"

"Right away."

Father and son turned and headed for the ranch house.

Tyler got on his cell phone. He called his brothers Teddy and Trevor and his father, who brought his two teenage brothers, Kyle and Kurt, and several uncles. Within thirty minutes they had a horse trailer and equine stretcher and enough McCabe men to move the tranquilized horse with the immobilized leg back to Healing Meadow.

Once back at the hospital barn, Tyler and his vet techs worked to x-ray and set the broken leg bone. They rigged the stallion with an immobilizing harness that lifted him a foot off the ground, hence keeping all the pressure off the injured leg.

Finally, it was just Susie and Tyler.

"You should really go on home," Tyler said, noting it was nearly three in the morning. Susie still looked great. Her hair was mussed, her amber eyes rimmed with fatigue. But like the Energizer Bunny, she kept right on going. What amazed him even more, was his reaction to her presence. He'd been really glad she was with him tonight. It had helped, having her nearby.

Susie edged closer, a comforting smile tugging

at the corners of her lips. "Are you going to sleep in the hospital barn tonight?" Susie asked softly.

Tyler nodded. Weariness settled in him, weighting his limbs. He rubbed at the tense muscles at the back of his neck. "Catastrophe'll probably sleep most of the night, but I want to be around in case there are any problems. My regular vet techs can take over in the morning." Tyler walked her as far as the barn doors. Outside, a black cat could be seen near the corner, lapping from a saucer of milk. When the cat saw the two of them, it disappeared off into the night once again.

Tyler turned back to Susie. He took her hand, squeezed it fondly. Wanting her to know how much she meant to him, he looked into her eyes. "Thanks for staying."

Susie flushed and dropped her head shyly. "I didn't do much."

Realizing he was still holding her hand, and didn't want to let it go, Tyler reminded himself the two of them weren't dating, no matter how intimate this evening had felt. He forced himself to untangle their fingers, step back. He shoved his hands in the pockets of his vet scrubs. "You made coffee and sandwiches for the men."

Susie compressed her lips. Unhappiness permeated her low tone. "I had to do something to keep myself from going back over to the Rooney ranch and punching both father and son out."

Tyler nodded. "I had a little trouble controlling myself, too."

Susie sighed, shook her head. "How do you stand it?"

Aware she'd hit on the worst part of his job, Tyler stepped out into the silent November night and shrugged. "It goes with the territory. Kindness and concern can sometimes be in short supply, especially when it comes to animals."

Susie's blond hair gleamed in the circle of light around the barn. "But to treat a beautiful stallion like Catastrophe as if he were completely expendable..." Her voice caught. She couldn't go on.

"It happens." More often than Tyler liked to admit. He was just glad he had been there to stop it. Although, had it been any of the partners in his veterinary practice, he was certain they would have reacted the same way he had.

Susie ran her index finger and thumb beneath her eyes. "Catastrophe is lucky he has you."

"And you, from the looks of it."

Unaware it was all he could do to keep from taking her in his arms and holding her close, Susie took a deep breath, shoved her hands in the pockets of her skirt. She looked in the direction Catastrophe was quartered, then back at Tyler. The edge of her teeth worried her soft bottom lip. "What will happen to him once he's well?" she asked.

Tyler relaxed. This much, at least, was already figured out. "I'll give him to my brother Teddy. He can use him as a stud on his horse ranch."

Just that quickly, Tyler saw the invisible force field going up around her emotions.

Even as he admired the inner toughness and tenacity that had helped Susie survive all life's hardships, he wished she would lean on him a little more. Wished she would let him in...instead of allowing him only so close, and no closer....

Tyler studied the new sheen of moisture in her eyes. Maybe he should have taken her in his arms and held her close. "Are you going to be okay?" He was used to veterinary emergencies. She wasn't. Maybe this evening's events had been more traumatic for her than she had let on.

Susie mustered up a smile, all easy grace once again. She shoved her hands through her hair. "Just tired. Speaking of which...tomorrow's a workday." She turned and headed for her pickup truck. "I really better go on home."

"I DON'T GET WHAT YOU'RE so upset about," Amy told Susie the next morning as the two of them unloaded flats of autumn flowers from the flatbed truck used to transport Amy's product.

"So Tyler plans to give Catastrophe to his

brother Teddy, to use in his horse-breeding operation? Why is that bad?"

Why indeed? Susie wondered, stopping to admire the quality of the chrysanthemums Amy had grown on her ranch.

Looking like a petite blonde pixie, with her short, cropped blond hair, Amy pushed a full cart into the store. Susie followed suit.

"He does it all the time, doesn't he, with animals that come to his practice that—for whatever reason—no longer have a home."

Susie began stacking items on empty shelving next to the Thanksgiving wreaths. She thought back to the emotional events of the evening before.

"I guess last night was the first time I actually saw him interacting with one of those animals." Susie turned to her most sentimental sibling, knowing if anyone would understand her concern, it was Amy. "Tyler seemed to really feel something for Catastrophe. Something special. And then, once the crisis was passed, and everything was cool again, he just…turned it off."

Amy lifted a thoughtful brow. "Like he does with you?"

Susie flushed. "Excuse me?"

Finding it impossible to stand still a moment longer, she pushed her empty cart back out to the truck.

Amy helped Susie unload decorative gourds and pumpkins from the truck. "You and Tyler both seem to have on-off switches for each other. Maybe that's what is really bothering you."

Susie filled her cart, then rolled it over to the front of the store. "You've been watching too much *Dr. Phil* on TV."

Amy grinned, guilty as charged. "I learn a lot from that show."

"Such as?" Susie lined up the gourds in a neat row.

Amy concentrated on arranging the pumpkins in a welcoming display of autumn bounty and only when she'd finished, turned and put a gloved hand on her hip. Her dark brown eyes were serious. "We all need a soft place to fall, Suze. For years now, Tyler's been your soft place to fall. And I get that. I see the way he is whenever you're having a rough time. And vice versa. What I don't get is why in between the challenging times of your lives, the two of you barely hang out."

Was it getting hot outside or what? Susie wondered.

Ignoring her baby sister's probing gaze, she returned to the flatbed. "We don't hang out all the time because Tyler and I are not like you and Teddy. Best friends forever and all that."

Amy rolled her cart up onto the truck, toward the back, for easier loading. "Then what are you?"

"Crisis buddies."

"Hmm."

"What does that mean?" Susie demanded, beginning to feel downright irritable.

Amy regarded Susie steadily. "It means maybe Mom and Dad are right," she said quietly. "Maybe it's finally time you started asking for more out of life than just surviving."

Emotion welled up inside Susie. Before she could stop herself, the resentment, long withheld, came pouring out. "You only think that way because you've never really had to battle for your life."

Amy looked so stricken, Susie felt ashamed.

She clapped a hand to her mouth. Tears welled. "Oh, Amy, forget I said that. I didn't mean it. I swear."

"No." Amy's voice was thick, emotional. Looking as though she might cry, too, she swallowed hard and got it together. "You're right. I *haven't* been through what you have." There was a little hitch in her voice. Teardrops fell over her lashes. "But I went through another kind of hell, watching you fight for your life, knowing there wasn't much of anything I could do except stand by and wait and watch and pray that everything would turn out all right eventually, which it did. In that sense, at least, you had it easy because you could do something to influence the outcome. You could fight for your life!"

"You're right of course. I—I'm sorry. I don't know what's gotten into me lately." She was feeling all tied up in knots.

Amy hugged her fiercely. "Don't be sorry. Just try really *living* for a change. And you can do it by giving those dates that Mom and Dad arranged for you a real chance."

Susie stepped back with a defiant sniff. "Hey." She thumped her chest. "I've met the first two."

Amy gave her a knowing glance. "And promptly discarded them, the second with Tyler McCabe's help."

Susie rolled her eyes and went back to loading plants. "Like you won't do the same when you're up for five fix-ups, courtesy of the folks."

Amy released a wistful sigh. "At this point, with me fast approaching thirty, and no husband and baby in sight," she admitted with a pragmatic wink, "I'm beginning to think the more the merrier when it comes to meeting potential soul mates. Although I haven't given up finding that special someone all on my own. The difference between me and you and Jeremy is that I am actively looking, and in fact, have never stopped."

Susie wasn't surprised about that. Amy always had been an incurable romantic, and would already be married with three kids by now if she had only met "The One." "Well, you'll be happy to know I'm seeing my second 'arranged introduction' for the second time later this evening," Susie reported.

Amy perked up. "It went that well, hmm?"

"Let's just say Gary Hecht and I had more in common than I expected." Gary loved numbers, and there were times when such a deep understanding of statistics and probability came in handy. But Amy didn't know Susie's intentions with her suitor and her expression said Amy was already planning Susie's wedding....

"What about the others?" Amy asked.

"My meet and greet with Bachelor Number Three is this afternoon. That's going to be a real date this time, not just thirty minutes of conversation."

Amy recoiled in shock. "How did that happen?" she demanded.

Susie smiled. "Let's just say Hal Albert called this morning and made me an offer I can't refuse."

"Of course I'll take Catastrophe off your hands when the cast comes off and he's ready for physical therapy," Teddy said, when he and Tyler talked in Tyler's office later that day.

Although Tyler specialized in large animals, he also cared for house pets when his partners in the practice were overbooked or out of town. Today was one of those days. And though normally Tyler didn't mind working in the vet clinic instead of the pasture or barn, today was one of those days when he felt really hemmed in, stuck inside a building.

Today, he'd rather be outside.

With Susie…

Whatever that meant.

Aware his brother was looking at him curiously, Tyler forced his mind back to the injured horse. "It'll be another six weeks or so before we can move him to the Silverado, depending on how fast Catastrophe heals."

Teddy had been in the horse-breeding business long enough to expect that would be the case. "Sure you don't want to keep him yourself?" Teddy asked casually.

Why did everyone keep asking him that? Tyler wondered irritably, as he led the way back to the rear of the building, where his next patient awaited. "If I wanted to keep him for myself, I wouldn't have just asked you if you wanted him," Tyler told Teddy in exasperation.

"Okay." Teddy surrendered with a lift of his palms. He watched as Tyler greeted a stray puppy that had been brought in earlier in the day and removed him from the holding cage where he'd been put, until attention could be paid. "You don't have to bite my head off."

"Sorry." Tyler started his exam. From the looks of the skeletal mutt, she had been dumped in the countryside and left to fend for herself.

Fortunately, the terrier-beagle mix had a really cute face and a winning personality and had already been claimed by the office receptionist's sister, who had just lost her border collie to old age.

"So what's really bothering you—if not the horse?" Teddy persisted.

Tyler turned his attention to a thorn in the dog's paw. Motioning to Teddy to hold the pup's lower half still, he steadied her chest and injured paw with one hand, and removed the thorn with a pair of tweezers. The paw looked red and angry where the thorn had been. Tyler applied an antiseptic-antiobiotic-numbing spray, then took a closer look at the wound. It seemed to require no other care for the moment. "What makes you think anything's bothering me?"

"Perhaps the fact you're grouchy as all get-out."

Tyler turned his attention to the pup's ears, which looked as if they had half a ton of dirt in them. "I didn't have a lot of sleep last night."

"I've seen you without sleep before." Teddy

leaned against the wall. "You usually handle it a lot better."

Tyler batted his lashes in a parody of a Southern belle. "Keep up the compliments and you'll give me a swelled head."

"Which has me wondering," Teddy continued with a knowing grin while Tyler cleaned the mutt's ears, "if this foul mood of yours has something to do with Susie Carrigan."

Finished, Tyler reached into the cabinet to get the first of several vaccinations the pup needed.

"What about Susie?" Tyler asked casually, giving the pup her shots.

Teddy shrugged. "I thought it might be hard for you, seeing her dating like there's no tomorrow."

Tyler went to the cupboard and retrieved a can of puppy food with nutritional supplements. He popped it open, dumped it onto a small paper plate and set it down on the floor next to the mutt. "First of all, there is no reason for me to object if Susie Carrigan wants to go out with guys other than me. We're the kind of buddies who help each other out in emergencies. That's all."

Teddy looked skeptical. "If you say so."

Tyler sure as hell did. "Second of all," he continued, aggravation increasing. "What the devil are you talking about?"

"Susie's got two dates today."

Irritated Susie hadn't mentioned either to him, but pleased she was dispensing with the potential boyfriends so quickly and efficiently, Tyler shrugged. "I imagine she wants to get the introductions over with so Meg and Luke will stop nagging her about settling down."

Teddy scoffed. "That wasn't the impression I had. In fact, Amy told me Susie was really excited about meeting Hal Albert at the Laramie Airfield."

THE ADVANTAGE OF BEING a McCabe in Laramie, Texas, meant there was no shortage of family. Tyler had relatives in every type of business in the area, including the airstrip.

Luckily for him, his cousin Will McCabe was working in the office of his charter jet service, instead of out flying a client to another destination.

Married after years of being single, the forty-two-year-old ex-navy pilot was the poster boy for happy family man.

Will greeted Tyler with a hug and a slap on the back. "What brings you out here?"

Curiosity. "I was in the neighborhood and thought I'd drop by and see what's going on out here."

Will smiled. "That sudden urge to say howdy wouldn't have anything to do with Susie Carrigan, now would it?"

Tyler accepted Will's offer of a seat. "She's here?"

"Not anymore." Will walked over to the printer, spewing out pages. "She left with Hal Albert."

"I don't think I know him."

Will grabbed a stack of papers out of the tray and headed back to his desk. "Hal's a skydiving instructor in San Angelo. He's looking into opening a school out here, if he can get enough interest."

If the McCabes and the Carrigans thought highly of Hal Albert, he had to be a nice guy. That did not in any way explain the jealousy roiling around in Tyler's gut. "Did Hal say where they were headed?"

Will nodded and pointed to the sky.

Okay, so Hal had taken Susie up in a plane.

That was no reason to wig out.

Tyler pretended an ease he could not begin to feel. "They seem to be hitting it off?" he asked casually.

Will shrugged. "No clue. All I can tell you is that Susie took off with Hal in his private plane a few hours ago and I haven't seen them since."

Which could mean they'd flown off to another destination. Or had engine trouble. Or were just flat-out having such a good time they weren't going to come back to the airstrip anytime soon.

None of the notions appealed to Tyler. "Do you know when they'll be back?" Tyler asked.

Will shook his head. "Neither Susie nor Hal left an estimated time of arrival with me."

Tyler frowned, knowing even as Will spoke that this was none of his business. As Susie had pointed out to him recently, he was not her chaperone. She'd call him if and when she needed him. When she didn't, it was his job to bow out like the Texas gentleman he was.

So why was that just about the hardest thing he had ever done?

Will gave Tyler a long, considering look. "Want me to leave her a message from you?"

Tyler exhaled, slowly and deliberately. "No. That's okay. I've got to get going anyway." He stood up and left.

"JEALOUS," SUSIE REPEATED TO Will McCabe, an hour later.

Will waved at Hal Albert, who was already taxiing his small private plane back to the end of the airstrip for takeoff.

Hal returned the salute.

Will turned back to Susie, smug masculine amusement shimmering in his eyes. To her discomfit, the ex-navy pilot looked as though he knew something Susie didn't. "It sure looked that way to me," Will drawled.

"Well, you're wrong." Disbelief racing through her, Susie planted her boots on the edge of the tarmac. The Texas wind made the brisk November afternoon even colder. "Tyler can't be envious of Hal." It didn't make any sense.

Will shrugged and lifted a dissenting brow. He turned the collar of his leather flight jacket up against the cold. "If you say so."

"I mean, why would he be?"

Tyler had never said one word about wishing he knew how to fly. Nor had he ever mentioned any desire to go skydiving. To her, anyway.

"They're both professional men. Successful," Susie continued theorizing out loud.

"I don't think my cousin's unhappiness had anything to do with careers," Will interrupted drily.

"Then what was—is—at the heart of it?" Susie demanded.

Will merely smiled at Susie as if she ought to know the answer to that.

He started walking with her toward the hangar, where the private jets were kept. Susie shivered, wishing she'd thought to bring her sheepskin lined suede cowgirl jacket with her, instead of just a sweater. She slanted another curious, assessing look at the charter air service owner. "You sure there was no emergency?" she pressed anxiously. "Family or vet or whatever?"

A roar sounded behind them as Hal's plane raced down the runway and took off.

Will's mood shifted from amused to perplexed. "He didn't say anything to that effect."

"Well, something must be wrong," Susie declared, her pulse beginning to race. "Otherwise, Tyler would not have come all the way out here looking for me in the middle of a workday."

Will looked Susie over from head to toe, before returning his eyes to her face once again. "Are you two dating?"

"No."

Will pursed his lips together thoughtfully. "Does he *want* to date you?"

What was it with everybody she knew suddenly matchmaking for her? And worse yet, fixing her up with Tyler McCabe? A man who had never shown the slightest interest in having that kind of relationship with her!

Susie shook her head and shoved her hands through her hair. She grumbled bad-temperedly, "Don't be ridiculous." *Don't get me wishing for the impossible, too!*

Will mulled that over. "Huh."

The heat of embarrassment climbed from Susie's neck to her cheeks. "What does 'huh' mean?" She hated it when men refused to just come out and say what was on their minds.

Will clamped a brotherly arm on Susie's shoulder. "I think you're putting your questions to the wrong guy. Go find Tyler. Ask him."

If only to satisfy her own mounting curiosity, Susie decided to do just that.

Luckily, he wasn't hard to find. By the time she reached the vet clinic, office hours were over and everyone else had left for the day. Only Tyler's pickup truck was in the lot.

The front door hadn't been locked yet so Susie strode in.

Tyler came around the corner, Dictaphone in hand. Clad in his usual snug jeans, custom-fitted boots and solid-colored cotton shirt, he looked so ruggedly handsome and sexy she felt herself go weak in the knees.

"Is everything okay with Catastrophe?" Susie's words came out in a rush. She dropped her shoulder bag and keys on one of the wooden benches in the reception area. "Will said you stopped by the airstrip this afternoon, looking for me." Breathlessly, she closed the distance between them. "What's going on here, Tyler?"

He gave her a look of choirboy innocence that was as unexpected as it was suspect. "I heard you were on a date and thought you might need some discreet help getting rid of Bachelor Number Three."

His casual confession left her feeling more disappointed than relieved.

Aware Tyler was waiting for an update, Susie recited dutifully, "Hal Albert turned out to be pretty nice. He's ex-military and he has his own skydiving instructing business, which he started from the ground up."

Tyler headed past her and locked the door. He turned the Closed sign around, and switched off the lobby lights. Hand beneath her elbow, he steered her toward the back of the building, where lights still blazed.

His whole body taut with tension, he dropped the Dictaphone next to the stack of files on his desk. "So you two have a lot in common."

"Actually," Susie made no effort to hide her surprise about that, "we do. We talked a lot about the pros and cons of being sole proprietors. He gave me some tips on how to expand into San Angelo if I ever have a mind to, and I told him how to go about getting a toehold in Laramie. He also offered to give me free skydiving lessons."

Tyler did not appear as if he wanted to imagine Susie leaping out of a plane and tumbling through the sky. He lounged back against the opposite wall, one booted foot across the other, his body at an angle. His eyes glittered with a mixture of doubt and cynicism that stung. "What are you going to give him in return?"

Not about to let Tyler think he had the right to rein her in, any more than her family did, Susie said, just as casually, "The pleasure of my company." End of story. End of his third degree!

He gave her a faintly baiting look. "No landscaping or plants?"

Susie stared at Tyler in confusion. "No. Although if he needed my help in that regard I'd be happy to work something out with him." Susie paused, her exasperation with him building. "And as long as we're playing twenty questions, why do you have that cynical look on your face?"

Their gazes locked, held. "No reason."

"Bull." Ignoring the butterflies in her stomach, she edged closer. "You're thinking something. You're just afraid to tell me what it is."

He flashed her a sexy half smile, even as worry darkened his hazel eyes. He pushed away from the wall, and edged closer, too. "I wouldn't say 'afraid.'"

"If you're not chicken," Susie baited, planting both her hands on her hips, "then tell me what's on your mind."

For a long moment, she thought he was not going to reply.

Tyler's glance narrowed. "The odds are companionship is not all he's wanting."

Susie's mouth opened in a round of surprise. "Hey!" Susie cautioned, incensed.

He adapted a no-nonsense stance. "I call 'em like I see 'em."

"Obviously." Susie treated Tyler to a withering glare before continuing sarcastically, "Although since you and he have never met each other, I hardly think you're an expert on what may or may not be motivating Hal Albert."

Tyler dropped his arms, came closer yet. Abruptly, his expression was conciliatory. "Look, Susie, I know how guys around here operate when it comes to you. They all handle you with kid gloves because they know what you've been through."

Susie frowned. "For your information, Hal not only knows what happened to me but he had his own bout with serious illness. Like me, he's now living one day at a time."

"Mmm-hmm."

Her resentment simmered. "Obviously, you've concluded there is something nefarious about that, too."

"All I'm saying is that one look at you—particularly for someone who is only living in the here and now—and there is only going to be one thing on his mind."

Susie marched away from him, not stopping until the desk stood between them. "I hate to tell you this, but you're not helping your case."

He circled his desk, too, his expression impatient. "I'm not trying to help me, Suze. I'm trying to help you. I'm trying to point out that your parents' well-intentioned meddling might have left you feeling a little vulnerable, especially now, around the holidays."

Susie could not deny that, much as she wanted. "And you think that makes me susceptible to seduction," she guessed.

Ty's mouth twisted. He braced his hands on his waist, his elbows jutting out in angry wings. "It's a mistake both of us have made before."

With each other.

Susie felt a stab of unexpected jealousy that left her feeling more uncertain and off-kilter than before. She told herself it was none of her business, but in the end she couldn't let it go. "You're saying you've turned to other women the same way you've turned to me, in the past?"

"Hell, no," Tyler said. He took her by the shoulders, forcing her to look at him. "When I'm miserable, Suze, the only person I want with me is you."

Talk about a backhanded compliment!

She extricated herself from his light, staying grasp and shoved her hands through her hair. "Now if only you could want me around when things are good, too," she found herself saying wryly, before she could stop herself.

Some emotion she couldn't quite define flickered in his eyes before another silence fell, this one even more awkward.

More telling…

And all the while, Tyler looked as if she had pushed him into the pool, from behind.

"Are you saying you want us to be more than time-of-trouble buddies?" he asked her eventually, in a low, cajoling voice. He paused to search her eyes. "That you want us to be the kind of friends that see each other all the time?"

Was that what she wanted? What had been missing in her life?

Susie knotted her hands in front of her, wishing she hadn't started this, but unable to back off, nevertheless. "Yes," Susie said slowly, deliberately. "That's exactly what I want."

Chapter Five

There's no time like the present.

"Then let's start tonight," Tyler said, taking both of Susie's hands in his.

"I wish I could but…" Susie let out a slow breath and looked at her watch.

Tyler smiled at her as if it were no big deal, when to him it *was* a very big deal. "Got another engagement?" He gave her a playful look.

Susie bit her lip, her face turning a self-conscious pink. "As a matter of fact…I do."

Telling himself he'd already done the unwarranted jealousy thing today, Tyler searched for some inner nobility that would give her what she needed in a friend while satisfying his need to forge a deeper connection with her.

"Is this an engagement where three's a crowd?" he asked her casually, reminding himself that, as friends, they would still be dating other people.

As pals, it was expected they would support each other's conquests and involvements.

"Six, actually," Susie answered, looking happier than he had seen her in a while as she gazed down at their enmeshed hands, "but who's counting."

She released her hold on him and stepped back, all cordial Texas grace. "And of course you can come along with me if you wouldn't mind going to the hospital to see Emmaline and her parents and Gary Hecht."

"The actuary?" The guy she'd barely been able to spend thirty minutes with at the driving range the other night?

"Yes." Susie smiled, looking relaxed, content and not the least bit starry-eyed.

Susie waited for Tyler to turn off the lights, then walked out the side door with him into the crisp autumn evening.

"I told him about Emmaline the night we were at the driving range, and since he consults with insurance companies all the time, he started rattling off facts and figures that showed just how futile it is to spend your life worrying about how you're going to die. I spoke with her parents. They gave me facts about Emmaline's illness. Gary compiled a whole host of statistics that showed just how high the odds are that she's not only going to survive this, but go into permanent remission. He ran them by her folks this morning at their home. Mr. and Mrs. Clark realized what a boost this would be to Emmaline's spirits and agreed to let him go to the hospital this evening and talk to her about his findings. I'm supposed to be there, too, and I'm going to be late if I don't get a move on."

Tyler clasped her wrist before she could head for her own pickup truck.

"Why waste gasoline? I'll drive us both, and bring you back to get your vehicle later."

Susie leaned into his easy grasp. "Okay."

Tyler was glad to see the evening with Gary Hecht, Emmaline and her folks went as well as Susie had predicted.

By the time Emmaline realized the odds were actually higher she would survive to her nineties, than succumb while still in her teens, she was in a much better frame of mind.

"I'm getting out of here tomorrow morning," Emmaline told Susie and Tyler after her parents had left to walk Gary down to the hospital lobby.

"That's great." Susie smiled.

Emmaline fingered the scarf around her head. "I know you're busy, but I was sort of hoping we could get started planning the landscaping of my backyard."

"Sounds great," Susie enthused. "The first order of business, now that you've had a chance to fig-

ure out what kind of plants and shrubs and flowers you like, is for me to see the yard at your home
and figure out what we've got to work with."

"When do you think you could stop by?"

Susie mentally ran down her schedule. "Tomorrow evening okay with you?"

Emmaline nodded. "Tomorrow's great."

"I'll check with your parents tomorrow and set
up a time," Susie said.

"Awesome." Emmaline gave them the thumbs-
up.

Tyler and Susie said good-night to the teenager,
and headed outside.

"What's the matter?" Susie asked as they
cleared the automatic doors and walked across
the parking lot. Visiting hours were ending. Others were headed to their cars and trucks, too.

Tyler shrugged and tried to summon up what
little gallantry he seemed to have left. "Nothing."

Susie squinted at him, intuitive as always. "You
look like you just lost your best friend."

*Maybe the opportunity to make her his best
friend.*

With a disgruntled frown, Tyler admitted, "I
was hoping we could spend tomorrow night together." Hoping that doing so would ease the unwarranted selfishness he'd been feeling the last

few days. Let them return to normal. Make that the "new" normal, he amended silently.

"We can," Susie enthused, chipper as always when everything was going her way. She caught his hand and swung their clasped palms between them. "Just come with me when I go see Emmaline."

Tyler caught the way-too-innocent sparkle in her eyes and grinned right back. He tightened his fingers over hers, and tugged her close before she could glide away once again. "I know what you're doing."

Susie paused next to the passenger door of his pickup truck. She leaned against the handle, looked up at him.

"You do?" she murmured softly.

Clearly, she did not believe it.

Tyler planted a hand on the roof of the truck, just left of her head. Aware their voices were carrying a little too much in the brisk night air, he leaned in close enough to inhale the fragrance of her skin and hair. "You're just trying to rope me into helping you dig up and replant the Clarks' yard."

Undeterred, Susie stuck her hands in the pockets of her suede jacket and ran the toe of her sturdy leather boot across the ground. "I'm that transparent, hmm?"

Tyler watched the swish of her long skirt just above her ankles, and marveled how feminine she was, at heart. "Absolutely."

"Next question then." Susie waggled her eyebrows at him. "Is it working?"

Tyler let his gaze rove from the playful curve of her lips, back to her eyes. Staying on the "just friends" side of the line was going to be more challenging than he had figured.

Aware she was awaiting his verdict on her clever machinations, he replied, "Yes, Suze, your little ploy is working to get me further involved with your good deeds." And every other kind, Tyler realized wistfully. It didn't seem to matter what Susie was up to. He wanted to be a part of it.

"Good! I think I'm going to like this change in our relationship," she announced with a flirtatious toss of her silky blonde head.

Tyler held the door for her and gave her a boost up into the cab.

"Why?" he teased, unable to help but note how pretty and sassy and right she looked, sitting in the passenger seat of his truck. "Because you think you'll have me wrapped around your little finger?"

Susie threw back her head and laughed, the sound soft, musical, and desire provoking. "Because I *know* I will."

"You really didn't have to pick me up," Susie told Tyler the next evening. "We could have met at the Clark residence."

Tyler shrugged. "I figured it would be easier on

them if their guests arrived together." Plus, Susie as everyday friend, instead of crisis buddy and or crisis lover, was going to take some getting used to. He figured the sooner they practiced their new roles, the sooner he would stop contemplating the fact that, as casual friends, they would never be making love again, even if a crisis did arise.

"You're right." Susie strode out the door of her house, as if them being together were the most natural thing in the world. "But I'm driving."

Tyler paused.

Susie frowned at his hesitation. "You drove last night," she reminded impatiently.

Yes. He had.

His fingers tightened on his truck keys.

"I just assumed…since I'm the guy…"

Temper flared in her amber eyes. "I can drive, too."

"I know that," Tyler countered, upset she thought this was a competency issue with him when it clearly wasn't. "But uh…" He struggled to find a way to word it without offending her, even as she strode away. "Usually…"

Susie rounded on him. "Usually nothing, Tyler McCabe." She propped both her hands on her waist and tossed her head in indignation. "If we're going to start hanging out together more then we have to establish new ground rules for how it's going to go. And the first of those is that I'm going to drive fifty percent of the time, and you're going to drive the other half."

What could Tyler say to that? It wasn't as if they were dating. If she were a guy friend, instead of a female friend, they would split the driving.

Aware she was already vaulting behind the wheel, he climbed in the passenger seat.

Unlike his extended cab pickup truck, which had a bench seat in front and back, hers had bucket seats in the front, and a bench in back.

The bench was cluttered with what looked like half her closet—a pile of CDs, two umbrellas, a big portfolio, a large sketch pad and pencil set, and a stack of books on trees, shrubs, annuals and perennials.

"Don't say a word," Susie muttered as she caught him looking at the mess.

Tyler realized this was the first time he had actually been in her truck. For whatever reason, they had always taken his.

"You've got clothes and stuff in yours."

Tyler always traveled with a clean shirt or two, a pair of jeans, clean coveralls and his vet bag. It made sense with the kind of work he did.

Susie started her engine and backed out of her drive. "I'm planning to organize it eventually."

Realizing his knees were pressed against the

dashboard, he felt around the side of his seat until he found the electronic controls. "Now that sounds like a good quote for your gratitude journal," he drawled, positioning his seat back as far as it would go. He mugged at her comically. "'I'm planning to do it eventually.'"

Susie snorted and shot him a sidelong glance. "You're so funny."

Tyler tilted his head. "Or is that 'Never accomplish today what you can do tomorrow...'?"

"Hilarious!"

"I thought so." Tyler settled comfortably in his seat.

Maybe this wasn't such a bad deal after all. When he was driving he had to pay attention to the road. As a passenger, all he had to do was look at the driver. And what a sight she was.

She had fashioned her thick hair into a loose single braid that fell down her back. She was wearing one of her skirts again—the kind she always put on when she was meeting with potential customers. This one had a trim fit around the hips and was looser around the knees. She had on a pair of point-toed, high-heeled boots he didn't think he had ever seen, and a thick wool turtleneck sweater, perfectly in keeping with the recent drop in temperature. No necklace tonight but hoop earrings he found incredibly sexy dangled from her ears.

Realizing he was veering into dangerous territory, noticing everything about her this way, Tyler turned his attention briefly to the passing scenery. "How's the gratitude journal coming anyway?"

Susie emitted a soft sigh that lifted and lowered the curves of her breasts. "I've been working on some sketches for the cover." She paused, shook her head, her frustration evident. "But thus far nothing is working."

"Want me to have a look at them?"

"Would you mind?" Susie slowed down as they reached the entrance to the brand-new subdivision where the Clarks' home was located. "I really need an unbiased opinion."

Unbiased, huh? "I'm not sure I can be without prejudice," he said frankly. "I think everything you do is pretty terrific."

As she turned to him, he was inundated with a waft of her signature citrus and floral perfume.

"Just so you know, McCabe," she teased with a contented wink. "Flattery will get you nowhere with me." Susie pulled over to the side of the wide boulevard, put the truck in Park and hit the interior lights.

Telling himself that she hadn't done what he'd like to do—stop the vehicle so they could kiss again—Tyler shifted position to ease the building pressure at the front of his jeans and quipped,

"What's that? Another confession-inspiring quote for your journal?"

She reached around to get her shoulder bag and brought it back to her lap. "A statement of fact." She pressed her lips together ruefully. "I know my faults and shortcomings better than anyone—"

"Don't we all," Tyler reflected.

One of *his* had to be an inability to stop seeing Susie as a woman he'd once again like to bed...a fact that left him riddled with guilt.

They were supposed to be buddies here, nothing more.

Oblivious to the ardent nature of his thoughts, she opened her bag and brought out a handwritten set of directions to the Clark home. "So polite compliments don't work on me," she mused in a low, distracted voice.

"What about ornery ones?" Tyler couldn't resist asking, focusing once again on their repartee. Anything to turn off the need... "Do those work?"

"From you?" With a smile, Susie took a quick look at what she'd written, then switched off the interior lights. She looked deep into his eyes. Winked. "If they seemed sincere, they just might...."

SUSIE KNEW THEY WERE flirting. She just didn't know what to do about it. Flirting was something she didn't do with her male friends, lest they get the idea she was interested in them romantically. She hadn't done it in the past with Tyler because they'd usually come together under somber or difficult circumstances, when neither of them were in the mood for joking around. Yet flirting with Tyler tonight seemed as natural as breathing. Worse, it was making her think about all sorts of forbidden things, like kissing him again, holding him and or letting him hold her. From there, her thoughts naturally went to the times in the past when they had let what seemed appropriate in the moment guide them and ended up in bed together. As friends, they could no longer do that. No longer make excuses for the unbridled lust and need for comfort that had led them astray in the past.

They had to stay within the prescribed guidelines.

A feat that was obviously going to be harder for her than she had imagined... And yet, she didn't want to give up on the idea of spending time with Tyler. She wanted their relationship to move to a more comfortable place. She wanted to be able to rely on him day in and day out, and have him rely on her.

Which meant she had to respect their agreement and keep her attraction to him in check.

So, for the rest of the drive she let the conversation turn back to the landscape architecture options she intended to present to Emmaline and her parents that evening. Luckily, the recently built tract house the Clarks had just moved into was a mere half a block away.

As she and Tyler emerged from the truck, he whistled. "Wow. No wonder Emmaline is unhappy."

The small, square ranch house had only one tree in the front yard, and a shrub on either side of the front door. All the other homeowners on the street had put in extensive landscaping. The Clarks hadn't gotten around to it. But then, they were busy working jobs and caring for an ill teenager.

Knowing she had her work cut out for her, but glad she was going to be able to do something to help lift Emmaline's spirits, Susie walked with Tyler to the door.

The Clarks answered the bell promptly, their expressions anything but welcoming. "I'm sorry," Mr. Clark said. "We tried to call you but apparently you'd already left. This evening isn't a good time after all."

"Is Emmaline sick from the chemo?"

"No," Mrs. Clark replied. "The antinausea meds they've given her seem to be working."

"You may as well tell them." Emmaline stormed into the foyer. Her face was red and swollen from crying. "It's no secret that I don't have a friend left in the whole wide world!" Emmaline burst into tears again.

"She's been getting RSVPs from the slumber party invitations she sent out all day." Mrs. Clark looked every bit as miserable as her only child felt.

"Not one of her friends can come." Mr. Clark looked as if he wanted to punch something.

"Not can't. Won't," Emmaline corrected, sobbing all the more copiously. "They don't want to be around anyone with cancer! And I don't blame them. I'm such a downer."

Susie handed her sketch pad and pencils to Tyler, then wrapped an arm around Emmaline's shoulder. "Let's go sit down and talk about it," Susie urged the young girl gently, even as she gave Emmaline's parents a look that pleaded for a moment or two alone.

"I'll go make some hot cocoa," Mrs. Clark murmured, getting the hint.

"I'll help." Mr. Clark hurried after her while Tyler followed Susie and Emmaline into the living room.

"I'm really sorry your friends have deserted you," Susie said.

"I'm not really surprised, though," Tyler put in, his tone harder, less sympathetic.

Emmaline and Susie stared at Tyler in shock.

He shrugged. "It happens to a lot of people.

They get scared they'll say or do the wrong thing so they don't do anything, and figure by staying away they're helping you more than they would be if they were actually around, seeing you through your illness."

Emmaline sniffed, looking somewhat comforted. "So you don't think it's about them not liking me anymore."

Tyler knelt in front of where Emmaline was sitting on the sofa. "I think it's about them being scared of the possibility of death and then being ashamed and upset that they're scared. Trust me." Tyler looked Emmaline in the eye. "Your friends who have deserted you feel a lot worse than you do right now."

Emmaline's lower lip slid out in a contemplative pout. "Okay, so they're the ones in the wrong. I get that." She dabbed her eyes. "It still doesn't solve the problem of me not having any friends here in Laramie. And don't talk about trucking in people who are interested in making friends with me because I have cancer, either. 'Cause that is just as bad."

"I agree," Tyler said.

"So what are you suggesting Emmaline do?" Susie asked curiously. She could see Tyler had some plan up his sleeve....

Tyler smiled as if the answer were obvious.

"I'm suggesting she go about making friends the old-fashioned way, by coming to the first annual McCabe-Lockhart-Chamberlain-Carrigan-Remington-Anderson family Thanksgiving with her parents."

"QUICK THINKING AND A wonderful solution to the problem, cowboy," Susie told Tyler later on the drive back to her place.

Watching him deal with Emmaline had reminded Susie why she had wanted Tyler around when she was sick. He knew just when to be sympathetic and compassionate. Just when to get a person to stop feeling sorry for themselves.

Looking a lot more comfortable now than he did on the drive over, Tyler flexed his broad shoulders and propped one arm on the door rest. He draped the other across the seat behind her. "At last count there were going to be around 250 people at the gathering. All ages, all personalities. Emmaline and her parents will have the opportunity to make plenty of friends," he said.

Susie took a moment to think about that.

It had been a very good idea.

Slowing as they reached her street, she slanted Tyler a glance. The sheer size of him seemed to fill the cab. "You think our moms will mind the fact we expanded the guest list without checking with them first?"

"Nope." Tyler flashed an ornery grin. He turned toward her and asked, "What do you think about my chances of getting Mrs. Clark to make one of the pies on my list?"

Susie parked in front of her home and cut the ignition. "I'm sure Emmaline's mother would be happy to do it if you asked."

Tyler got out of the pickup. "But you don't think I should."

Susie met up with him at her front bumper. The porch light bathed them in a welcoming circle of soft yellow light. "If I have to make the gratitude journals for all the guests, you have to do some cooking."

"With your help," he reminded her.

No more anxious to end their evening than he, Susie nodded. "That was our deal. Besides, I'm sure our moms will think of something for the Clarks to contribute to the feast."

"Okay," Tyler conceded happily, "we'll let them handle it."

Susie rummaged in her bag for her keys. "Meanwhile, speaking of those gratitude journals. You still up for looking at the cover design?"

"A promise is a promise." Together, they went into the house. Susie switched on lights. Tyler settled on the sofa.

She dropped a stack of rough sketches in his lap,

rummaged in the kitchen and came back with a bowl of chilled red and green grapes.

"So what do you think?"

Tyler thumbed through drawings of pilgrims, turkeys, holiday tables brimming with food, an autumn wreath and a horn of plenty. "Actually, I like the sketch of the fall garden you're doing for Emmaline and her folks."

Susie hadn't considered anything like that.

She blinked, wanting to make sure she'd understood. "For the cover?"

"The mock-up has flowers, and gold and red leaves. It's peaceful and serene. Not something that people would be expecting or something that's already been done to death."

Susie shifted the bowl to his lap, and got up to retrieve the sketch he was talking about. "This one."

"Yes." Tyler's expression was reverent, admiring. "You could put some writing on the front."

Susie scribbled out, "A Laramie, Texas, Thanksgiving" across the top of the page. "Down here—" she indicated the bottom "—we could put the date."

"Works for me."

"Okay, then." Susie was filled with relief. "Now all I have to do is finish organizing the quotes for the top of each page of the journal and take it to the printer. And find some gold ribbon to bind the pages." Suddenly, the task she'd been dreading did not appear all that daunting.

She shifted the drawing aside, and took back the bowl of grapes. They munched awhile in silence.

Tyler appeared to be in no hurry to go home, nor was she in a rush to see him leave.

And yet there was an underlying tension between them. Questions she had yet to pose, but really wanted—needed—to ask.

Maybe because there was so much she still did not understand about him.

"By the way, you were really great with Emmaline tonight," she said.

He looked pleasantly surprised at the compliment. "Thanks."

Susie pushed on deliberately. "Watching you talk to her, I realized you'd make a really fantastic dad."

His brows knit together in a frown, confirming her opinion this was dangerous territory.

"I don't see marriage in my future," Tyler told her gruffly. He got up from the sofa and walked into the kitchen. He returned with a glass of tap water in hand. He studied her over the rim of his glass. "You know that."

"I know you've said it," Susie replied, remaining where she was with effort. Her fingers curved over the edge of the bowl. "Most bachelors think that way at the height of their independence. It's why they are single. But they usually end up changing their minds."

Tyler's expression turned stony. He sat down beside her and took another handful of grapes. "Not me."

Susie looked at the rock-hard thigh six inches from hers. "Afraid you'll be fenced in?"

Tyler propped his feet on her coffee table and stretched his long legs out in front of him. "Why do you care?"

Why indeed? Susie wondered.

Usually her philosophy was to live and let live.

She shrugged her shoulders aimlessly. "Because I know your family is the same as mine, in that respect. Having kids, loving them, taking care of them, is a vital part of being a McCabe or a Carrigan."

Tyler scowled and finished the rest of his water in a single gulp. "I can do that as an uncle."

Susie studied the implacable lines of his face. Usually, she was the one hiding her feelings, her secret shortcomings. Not tonight.

Tyler looked as uncomfortable as she did every time the subject of the "future" came up.

She turned toward him, her knee brushing his

muscular, jean-clad knee. "But why don't you want it for yourself?" she persisted.

He narrowed his hazel-green eyes at her. "Because I don't do anything I don't do well," he said mildly.

Susie exhaled in frustration. She leaned forward. "But you do have what it takes, Tyler. You just demonstrated that tonight."

He disagreed with a shake of his head and an averted glance.

"It's easy to do what needs to be done when you're not all that emotionally involved," he stated finally.

Susie supposed that was true. But…

"You care about Emmaline."

Tyler plucked the remote control off the coffee table. "I didn't say I didn't."

"But?" Susie watched him turn on the TV.

Tyler gestured nonchalantly. "I handle situations like this so well precisely because I don't let myself get too close."

Susie could attest to that. Whenever she and Tyler had gotten too close, he had backed away. Just as he had backed away after they'd made love.

At the time, she had thought it was her.

What if it wasn't? What if it was *him?* What if *he* was the one with intimacy issues? What if they *both* had them?

"Like with Catastrophe?" she asked cautiously at length, studying the emotionally shuttered look in his eyes. "You care about that horse," Susie continued, when a moment passed and he didn't respond. "I could swear you'd even like to keep him for yourself. But you won't."

"I'm his vet." Tyler started flipping channels. "I don't want to lose my objectivity."

Susie rolled her eyes at the age-old male aversion techique. "So you'll get him well, find a new home for him."

His expression turned even more unrelenting. "Teddy has already agreed to take Catastrophe when he's well."

"So you can forget about the stallion and get on with your life," Susie guessed.

Tyler settled on a recap of all the weekend football games. "Pretty much."

"Just like you've always done with me," Susie stated flatly.

TYLER DIDN'T KNOW WHAT to say. No one else had figured this out. No one else had dared question him on it. He turned off the television and shifted to face her, aware he was no closer to understanding her than she was to understanding him. "In the past, yeah, that's the way it was because we were crisis buddies. To be able to help you, I had to retain a certain distance."

"The same way most medical professionals do with their patients," she countered, looking both hurt and distressed.

"More or less," Tyler admitted, enjoying the challenging nature of the conversation the way he always did, when they went toe-to-toe on a subject.

Susie's teeth raked her lusciously soft lower lip. "All this time I thought…" Her voice caught. Pride—and possibly the fear of revealing too much about herself—kept her from continuing.

He caught her hand in his, as determined to uncover her secrets as she had been to wrest his from him. "You thought what?"

Susie gulped. "That you weren't interested in me in that way. That so far you weren't interested in any woman to the point where you wanted a real relationship. But that's not it at all, is it? It isn't that you haven't met The One For You. It's that you won't let yourself fall in love."

He loathed the accusation. "You're one to talk!" he scoffed.

Susie leaped to her feet. "I've had cancer!"

Tyler caught her hand and drew her right back down. "*Had* being the operative word."

"I may not have a future." Susie shifted position, so her knee was no longer resting against his thigh. "But, Tyler, you do. You could still have it all, if you'd let yourself."

He drew in a long, calming breath. "You don't get it."

Susie looked furious. "I'm trying!"

Tyler leaned forward and shoved both his hands through his hair. His clasped hands rested on the back of his neck. "I'm not like my mom or Travis, my adoptive dad. I'm like my birth father."

Twin spots of color appeared in her cheeks. "I thought he died when you were a kid."

"When I was eight," Tyler confirmed. "But he and my mom were married when my brothers and I were born. He couldn't handle triplets and he and my mom ended up getting divorced. Deep down, I'm just like him."

"How do you figure that?" Susie asked in a low, serious voice.

Tyler exhaled, caring about Susie too much to lie to her. "The summer I turned sixteen I got a job taking care of horses at this dude ranch in Colorado."

Her shoulders tensed. "I vaguely recall that."

It had been, Tyler recalled, before they'd gotten close.

"Everyone was envious of you. They thought it was such a cool job."

"I fell hard for the owner's daughter. Andrea

was sixteen, too, and we dated all summer." Tyler forced himself to remember, disillusionment filling his heart. Tyler reached over and took Susie's hand. "Shortly before I left, Andrea got really sick. She came down with a virus that attacked her heart." He stood and began to pace. "She was hospitalized and put on the transplant list." He clenched his teeth, embarrassed by what a heartless bastard he had been. "I couldn't handle it." Misery engulfed him now as it had then. "I completely bailed on Andrea and I didn't look back. She died a month later without ever hearing from me again."

"Oh, Tyler." Disappointment and sadness mingled in Susie's gaze.

He clenched his fists at his sides. "I realized then as much as I wanted to be like my adoptive dad, Travis, that in reality I was just like my real dad. When the going got tough, I got going."

"But when I got sick and all my friends deserted me, you stepped in, never once deserting me," Susie argued.

Not about to let Susie browbeat him into taking back his sentiments, Tyler said, "Because by then I had figured out the secret all the medical professionals use. To only let yourself care so much and never more. Enough to be compassionate and kind. Not enough to have your judgment threatened or to be so devastated if things don't work out the way everyone hopes they will that you can't go on."

Her expression changed. "So that's what you did with me," she concluded.

"Right," Tyler said.

But even as he spoke he wondered if that was still true. He'd always been able to keep his guard up before. Lately, when he was with Susie, the self-protective barriers had a way of coming down. He wasn't even aware of it. Suddenly, like now, he'd find himself confiding in her, talking about things he never discussed with anyone. If he weren't careful, he'd find himself wanting to be more than friends with her.

That'd be fine...as long as everything remained status quo. But if anything shifted, if things weren't okay...what would happen if he bailed on Susie the way he had bailed on Andrea?

Tyler knew he couldn't risk it.

Couldn't risk not being there for Susie however she needed him, whenever she really needed him.

He would not desert her the way he had Andrea.

"The point is, Suze, you deserve better than me," Tyler said, beginning to pace the length of the room once again.

"I'll tell you what I deserve," Susie said fiercely, leaping to her feet.

"And what's that?" Tyler demanded, impatient now to leave, before he revealed anything else about himself he didn't want her to know.

"Just wait and see," she murmured back, looking deep into his eyes.

And then her next move shocked the hell out of him.

Chapter Six

Live each day to the fullest.

All this time, Susie thought she had needed Tyler. She had never realized how much he needed her. Not just to celebrate a monumental event in his life when he was otherwise unattached and they'd had too many margaritas to be thinking straight, or when he was reeling with grief at the loss of a dear friend. Those moments had been important, but rare. This was different. Tyler had confided in her in a way he had confided in no one else.

The life that had seemed so limited in so many ways now exploded with possibilities and chief among them, Susie admitted to herself, was Tyler McCabe.

No longer just buddies who turned to each other in time of trouble or "comfort" or "celebratory" lovers, they were on the way to being everyday friends. And maybe, Susie thought, as she moved closer yet, wrapped her arms around Tyler's neck and brought her lips to his, so much more.

The last thing Tyler had expected when he'd brought Susie home tonight, was to be kissing her again. He sure hadn't expected her to get him to open up and then take the initiative. But now that they were in each other's arms again, now that her lips were moving beneath his, he found himself succumbing to the desire he had promised, for both their sakes, he would never resurrect again. The blood thundered through him, and he reveled in the soft surrender of her body against his. Yet he knew what he had to do.

With a groan of frustration, Tyler sifted his hands through her hair, tore his lips from hers. "Susie…"

She kissed his jaw, the skin behind his ear. "No talking."

Hands on her shoulders, he set her apart from him. As he stood looking at her, he could see the vulnerability in her amber eyes. Her lower lip, soft and pink and bare, was trembling slightly. Forcing himself not to think about kissing her again, Tyler said stoically, "We need to talk about this."

Twin spots of color brightened Susie's high cheekbones. Sensing what he was going to say but looking no less determined, she reached for the button on his shirt. "Then I'll just have to find ways to shut you up."

Knowing she needed to realize he had no intention of misleading her, he guided her back to the sofa, sat down and took her hands in his. "I'm serious."

Her eyes darkened with passion. "So am I." She slid over onto his lap and wrapped both her arms around his neck. "We've done enough talking, Tyler. Too much, really. Right now, I just want to feel."

Tyler directed his gaze away from the soft, inviting curves of her breasts. "This wasn't in the plan."

Susie swallowed, and continued looking at him as if she didn't know quite how to handle that pronouncement—or him. "I live moment to moment." She bit her lip. "I thought you knew that."

Wishing he hadn't been brought up to be inherently gallant, especially where ladies were concerned, Tyler studied the disarray of her blond hair, wanting to run his hands through its softness. Trying not to think how delectably sexy she was in or out of bed, he looked her straight in the eye and announced, "Making love with me is not what you need."

She lifted her chin, challenging him to try and chastise her for daring to live her life to the fullest in whatever cockeyed way she chose. "Suppose you let me be the judge of that," she said softly, smiling with a seductiveness that darn near broke his spirit.

Because, like it or not, he knew what he had to do. "No," he told her firmly, ignoring the flash of hurt and vulnerability in her expression. "I'm sorry, Suze. Much as I want to, I can't let us do this again."

SUSIE STARED AT HIM IN disbelief. She was sitting on his lap. She could feel the strength and heat of his arousal. And yet… "You're turning me down?"

Ever so gently, Tyler shifted her off of him and onto the sofa. He regarded her with steadfast care. "With a great deal of regret, yes, I am."

"Why?" She didn't know whether to kiss him or send him out the door.

"Because I'm not what you need," Tyler explained.

Temper exploded deep inside her. Ever since her illness she had hated it when her life veered out of control. It had never felt more so, than just now. "Not what I need or not what you want me to need?" She glared at him, forcing him to make the distinction.

He put up both hands in the age-old gesture of surrender. "Come on, Suze. Don't take this personally."

"Don't take it personally?" Susie picked up the bowl of grapes and marched toward her kitchen. She put the uneaten bounty back in the fridge and closed the door with as much bang as she could get out of the padded edges. She whirled back to face Tyler, her fists balled at her sides. "How in tarnation am I supposed to do that?"

"Friends don't make love."

Susie tried to act with a coolness she couldn't begin to feel. She leaned against the counter, facing him, and folded her arms in front of her. "That depends on the friends, don't you think?"

Tyler's bedroom eyes met and held hers again. "Sex complicates things."

Aware they were headed into territory much more intimate than if they had just made love and not bothered to dissect their motives and emotions, Susie replied, "It hasn't before."

Tyler settled opposite her. "Sure about that?"

Silence fell between them, unsettling, unbridgeable. Tyler's voice deepened compassionately, and he continued in a calm deliberate voice, "Or do you think it was a coincidence that, in the past, when we made love, we could barely look each other in the eye?"

She picked up a dish towel and pleated it between her fingers. Leave it to him to point out the downside. "Of course it was awkward."

He paused as if to reharness his emotions. "I'm tired of our relationship being awkward," he continued, jaw set.

Susie dropped the towel, not ready to give in just yet. "So let's end the weirdness," she suggested casually. "Let's agree we have a great physical chemistry and just act on it whenever the mood strikes."

Tyler tilted his head, as if actually considering it. "Make booty calls for each other," he rephrased.

"Yes."

Briefly, guilt flashed in his hazel eyes. "Your parents…"

"Have no say in this."

Tyler frowned and came closer. "Maybe not, but they want something much better for you, Suze. And so do I."

Restless, Susie opened up the dishwasher. She took out the clean dishes and began putting them away. Tyler was standing right beside her. The masculine scent of his skin and hair inundated her senses, making her want him all the more. Frustration boiled over inside her. Aware he was watching her, waiting for her response, she stopped what she was doing, as abruptly as she had started it, and turned her glance up to his. "You just told me you're never going to marry." She paused and wet her lips. "Did you mean it?"

Looking every bit as conflicted as she felt, he set his jaw and nodded. "Yes, I meant it. I am not and never will be husband material."

Susie caught him by the shirtfront and hauled him against her, taking charge of her feelings and the situation once again. "Well, I'm not wife material," she countered, just as seriously. Resolutely, she searched his eyes. "Does that mean I have to go through my whole life with the nonexistent sex life of a nun?"

He emitted a long lust-filled sigh, and gently ran his hands from her shoulders, down her arms, to her hands, eliciting tingles wherever he touched. "You still have two more guys to meet," he reminded her with obvious reluctance. "Maybe one of them will be the one."

Susie scoffed and said around the tightness of her throat, "Doubtful."

He squeezed their joined hands before disengaging them altogether. "You still have to give it a try." Gently, he touched her face, cupping her cheek with the flat of his palm. Painfully honest, his eyes touched hers. "Maybe in five or ten years if you still haven't met someone…"

Her emotions in turmoil, Susie walked away from him once again. "Now you're beginning to sound like my sister Amy and your brother Teddy, and their longstanding promise to have a child together if neither of them were married when they turned thirty."

He followed her to the opposite counter. "That was a joke. You know that."

"Maybe." Susie knelt to put a casserole dish in the cupboard, next to the kitchen sink. "And maybe not." Susie stood and went back to the dishwasher for the silverware caddy. "Amy's birthday is coming up soon. She's a little bummed about the prospect of being thirty and single."

Tyler watched as Susie dropped forks into the drawer. "I still think we need to give this 'just friends all the time' thing a try," he insisted.

Susie sighed and shot him one last persuasive glance. "You don't know what you're missing," she said.

Tyler looked into her eyes and this time it wasn't hard for her to read his thoughts. Tyler did know what he was missing. He even regretted the loss. That didn't, however, change his mind.

"THE THING IS, I FEEL like such a fool," Emmaline confided several days later when Susie went over with a truckload of plants.

Susie's landscaping crew had been over earlier to plow up the portion of the yard where the flowers and shrubs were to go.

"I should have known that things weren't going to work out the way I wanted," Emmaline continued, dropping bulbs in the wells Susie was fashioning.

"I know what you mean," Susie commiserated. Her life wasn't turning out the way she wanted, either.

Tyler hadn't called her.

She hadn't called him.

Susie didn't see the awkwardness that had sprung up between them once again going away anytime soon.

"You think you know someone…" Susie guessed where the conversation was leading.

Emmaline nodded. "…you think that person is your friend…"

"…and then find out you're not on the same page after all," Susie concluded sadly.

"How do you deal?" Emmaline asked, throwing up her thin arms. "I mean, you seem so together and everything."

It's all a farce.

Susie covered a bulb and smoothed the dirt with a trowel. Emmaline copied her movements with another bulb.

"I guess what you have to remember," Susie said eventually, doing her best to be a role model as well as a confidante and fellow survivor and friend to the ill teenager, "is that everybody has problems. It isn't a matter of whether you have any or not. It's just what specific problems you have, versus what specific problems someone else has."

Emmaline rested her face on her upraised knee, admiring the blooming chrysanthemums they had already planted. "I hadn't thought of it that way."

Finished with the bulbs, Susie began digging a spot for the ornamental grasses that would provide the border for the flower beds. "Yes, having cancer bites, but so does losing your job."

Emmaline grinned ruefully. "Or your hair."

"Speaking of which." Susie smoothed the dirt with her trowel and sat back on her heels. "I know you're not all that fond of the wig you were wearing—or maybe I should say, not wearing—in the hospital."

Emmaline put a hand up to her head, which was covered with a wool knit cap that while cute, only served to emphasize her baldness underneath. Susie knew how self-conscious she'd felt when undergoing chemotherapy. Bad enough she'd lost her eyebrows and eyelashes. She'd had to endure all the pitying stares from strangers who could tell at a glance she had cancer.

Emmaline made a face. "You noticed how dorky it is."

Susie saw no reason to pretend there wasn't a problem, when as far as Emmaline was concerned, there clearly was. "You could get your wig cut. I mean I had mine adjusted by a professional stylist a couple of times. It made all the difference in the way I looked and felt about it."

"It's still going to look fake because it's a synthetic."

Human hair wigs ran into the thousands, Susie knew. "You could wear the ones I wore when I was sick."

"You still have them?"

Susie removed several dwarf juniper bushes from their black pots and set them on the ground, next to where she intended to plant them. "Actually, I've got two of them." Both were extremely expensive and made of human hair. "My uncle, Beau Chamberlain, owns a movie studio and he was able to get them for me."

"And you never got rid of them?"

Susie shrugged. "It seemed like it would be tempting fate to get rid of them."

Emmaline rolled her eyes. "I know all about that. I'm afraid to make plans past the next few weeks."

"Anyway, I brought them with me, just in case you wanted to give them a try," Susie said. "They're in a box in my truck."

"Awesome."

"I should caution you, though. They're short, curly and blond—not long and red."

Emmaline grinned. "Even more rockin'. I always wanted to be a blonde, and now that I don't have any eyelashes or eyebrows, no one will know I'm not!"

Susie smiled.

She knew all about wanting to be someone or something else.

She'd felt that way when Tyler turned down her request they become lovers, too, instead of just friends.

"Looks like Catastrophe is on the mend," Teddy remarked, the next evening.

Tyler ran his hand down the stallion's mane, smiling as the big animal leaned into his touch. Though he'd done his best to keep a professional objectivity, having Catastrophe at Healing Meadow, knowing the horse had no owner to soothe him through the ordeal of being confined via harness and elevated to keep weight off the broken leg, had Tyler spending more time with his patient than he ordinarily would. Two of the nights, he'd slept in the hospital barn, and given the vet tech on duty an unexpected night off.

Tyler had told himself he was doing it because he wanted to make sure nothing went wrong in the initial recuperative process. The reality was he hadn't wanted to spend the night alone in his ranch house, thinking about Susie and the way everything had gone right, then wrong. He'd been trying to protect her by refusing to allow them to become physically intimate once again. She'd taken it as a rejection. To the point he feared their short-lived "friendship" might be over, and if that was the case, it was reasonable to expect their ability to call on each other in time of trouble was over, too.

What was that saying? Hell hath no fury like a woman scorned. And there was no doubt Susie Carrigan felt scorned.

"Earth to Tyler," Teddy teased.

Tyler stroked his hand down Catastrophe's sleek, well-muscled side.

"I don't know if I've ever seen you this distracted," Teddy continued. "Or this enamored of a horse. You sure you want to give Catastrophe up?"

Why did everyone keep asking him that? First Susie, then his vet tech, now his brother.

"What would I do with another horse?" Tyler asked, cutting an apple in quarters. "I barely have time to ride my own mount as it is."

"Only because you don't make time," Teddy countered. "And wouldn't it be nice to have a horse for a lady friend to ride, should you ever get a steady lady friend?"

Tyler offered the treat up on the palm of his hand. "You're a laugh riot."

"Just saying you could do with a little less work and a lot more social life."

"I'll take that under advisement." Tyler offered up another section of apple, smiling as Catastrophe demolished that, too. Tyler gave the horse another affectionate pat, then stepped out of the stall and headed down the aisle. Just outside the door, a black cat was examining a dish of kibble. "Catastrophe is a fine horse," Tyler continued, checking on his next patient, a mule recovering from a tangle with a barbed wire fence. "He's perfect for use as a stud. Which is why you should have him."

Teddy stuck his hands in his pockets and leaned against the stall. "If you still feel that way after he's finished recuperating, I'll take him."

"But…" Tyler prodded, checking on a row of stitches that had been flirting with infection.

Teddy shrugged. "That'll be weeks from now. By then, you may be so attached to Catastrophe you may not want to give him up. If that's the case, I'll understand."

Tyler rolled his eyes, as outside the door, the black cat took off like a bat out of hell. "Boy, you don't give up, do you?"

His brother smiled. "Let's just say I know how softhearted you are when it comes to animals who've not been appreciated the way they should have been." At the other end of the hospital barn, the vet tech on duty for the night walked in. Which explained, Tyler thought, why the people-shy cat had taken off like that.

Gabby Hayes was a twenty-year-old college student who wanted to be a large animal vet someday. Petite and darkhaired, with a lively sense of humor and a strong work ethic, she was everything he could have wanted in a part-time employee.

"You're not sending me home tonight," Gabby told Tyler before he could speak. "I need the experience. And you need the sleep."

The question was, would he be able to shut his eyes? Tyler wondered. Or would he just lie there, looking at the ceiling, thinking about Susie again?

Teddy laughed. "You tell him, Gabby. He doesn't listen to me."

Tyler shot his brother a look and grumbled, "With good reason. You're an idiot."

Teddy took the familial dig with the good humor with which it was given.

Gabby hung up her jacket and purse. Her expression turned serious. "Listen, Doc, I know you don't like to gossip, but I heard something today when I went in to my hairdresser's. I didn't want to ask anyone then, but I figured you might know. Has Susan Carrigan got cancer again?"

For a moment, Tyler thought he couldn't possibly have heard right. Teddy looked just as sucker punched as he felt.

"What makes you think that?"

Worry lit Gabby's eyes. "She took these two wigs in to get them cleaned and styled. Then she had her hair cut in the same short, curly style. Her stylist said something about not having seen the wigs since Susie was sick, years ago, and Susie said she hadn't looked at them, either. Then everybody got kind of quiet. And somebody said they were glad Susie was healthy now, and Susie kind of nodded, but she didn't say anything else about it, she just changed the subject."

Tyler's insides turned as cold as ice. The thought of anything happening to Susie was more than he could take.

Was that why...

Surely she hadn't known she was ill again when she asked him to make love to her. Or had she?

Aware both Teddy and Gabby were waiting for his answer, Tyler cleared his throat and said, "I haven't heard anything that would indicate Susie Carrigan was ill again."

Gabby relaxed slightly. "I hope not. She's such a nice person. Everybody buys their landscape plants and flowers from her."

Tyler paused to give Gabby updated instructions for the hospitalized animals care, then walked outside with Teddy. The two brothers exchanged mutually concerned glances.

"Amy said anything to you?" Tyler asked his brother.

Teddy shook his head. "No. And I know if Amy knew anything about her sister being sick that she would have said something. This is not the kind of news Amy would keep to herself."

"Unless the family wanted to keep it quiet for a while. Let Susie get through Thanksgiving without a lot of tea and sympathy." Tyler recalled how much Susie had hated the pitying glances of others, no matter how well meant.

Teddy clapped a comforting hand on Tyler's shoulder. "Look, if it were true, I'm sure Susie'd head straight for you."

Would she?

After the way they had parted the other night?

Tyler felt a sinking feeling deep inside, and more regret, fear and guilt than he could ever recall experiencing in his life.

"Call her. Find out what's going on," Teddy urged.

Tyler was already heading for the Healing Meadow ranch house. "I will."

The only problem was Susie wasn't answering her cell or home phone. Nor did she appear to be home. Finally, in desperation, Tyler called one of her employees at the landscape center, Mark Paggiano. "I'm trying to track down Susie."

"She went to Dallas for a few days."

Dallas. Where she had received her chemotherapy, years ago, because Laramie Community Hospital hadn't had an oncology unit then. Tyler fought to keep his voice casual. "Do you have a number where she is staying?"

"Actually, I do."

SUSIE FIGURED IT WAS MAID service, there to clean her room, when she heard the knock at seven-thirty the next morning. Reluctantly, she rolled out of bed, and padded barefoot across the plush carpet. Still yawning, she opened the door as far as the steel privacy cross bar would allow and blinked at what she saw. Six feet four inches of handsome Texan. Hazel eyes staring at her as if she were a ghost.

Susie blinked, sure she must be dreaming. Her heart rate picked up and she shut the door enough to take off the privacy lock. "What," Susie asked Tyler McCabe, ushering him in, "are you doing here?"

As the next thought occurred, her heart skidded to a stop, before resuming at a much quicker rate. "Everything's okay in Laramie, isn't it? I mean family, friends. No one's hurt or sick."

Tyler lifted a hand to let her know her concern for her loved ones was unwarranted. "Far as I know everyone there is okay." Tyler continued staring at her, his gaze roving her hair.

Remembering she'd had it cut and he hadn't seen it, she touched a hand to the tousled curls. When her hair was shoulder length or longer, the weight of it pulled it down into thick albeit somewhat unruly waves. When it was short like now, the curls came alive and formed springy corkscrews unless she went to the trouble of straightening it with an iron, which she had not done.

"Then why are you here?" Susie demanded, perplexed.

Catching sight of a businessperson on his way to a meeting, looking at Susie in her clingy tank top and low-slung pajama pants, Tyler shouldered his way in, shut the door behind him. "I need to talk to you."

Susie perched on the edge of her bed and rubbed the last of the sleep from her eyes. "Obviously. The question is why?"

Tyler checked out the remains of her minibar feast the night before.

"I want to make sure you're okay."

Susie got up and began collecting the candy bar wrappers and diet soda cans. She had always used chocolate and caffeine to comfort herself. Last night had been no exception. She balled them up and tossed them into the trash can. "Why wouldn't I be okay?"

Tyler sat down in one of the chairs next to the window. He leaned forward in a confidence-inspiring pose, forearms on his thighs. "You tell me."

Inexplicably, Susie felt as if she had landed in the middle of an episode of *Dr. Phil*. Arms crossed, she ignored his obvious desire she take the comfy club chair opposite him and kept her distance. "No. You tell me. Something brought you here. What was it?"

Tyler sat back and stretched his long legs out in front of him. "I heard you'd cut your hair in the same style as the wigs you used to wear when you were undergoing chemo."

Too late, Susie realized her current position had him at eye level with her exposed navel. "So?" She rummaged around in the minifridge behind her for another can of cola. She offered him one, he shook his head, refusing.

"I also heard you took the wigs in for cleaning and styling."

Susie popped the lid on her drink. She was too sleepy to be playing guessing games like this. "And then what?" She took a sip of the bubbly cola. "Someone alerted the media?"

Tyler seemed to be struggling with himself. Finally, he swept his hands through his rusty-brown hair, left them momentarily clamped behind his neck before dropping them to his lap again. Not once did he take his eyes off her face. "You'd tell me if you were sick again. Wouldn't you?"

Yet another bizarre question, way too early in the morning. Susie shrugged. "I don't know if I would or not, but I'm not, so…" Shivering in the cool air of the room, Susie caught a glimpse of herself in the bureau mirror, noticed her nipples were visible beneath the thin cotton top. She put her drink down on the top of the TV and went to the closet. She reached for a cropped cardigan she'd had on the day before, and slipped it on.

Tyler's eyes narrowed suspiciously. "Then why'd you cut your hair like that?"

Susie regarded him with mounting exasperation. What gave him the right to give her the third degree? Yet she knew the fastest way to get to the bottom of whatever was going on was simply to answer his questions. "I recalled how much I liked it this way, it's a cut that's coming back into style, and I hadn't worn it this way for years, so…" She went back to sipping cola, and letting the icy beverage energize her. "I went for it."

He stood and came closer. He hadn't shaved that morning, and the stubble of rusty-brown clung to his stubborn McCabe jaw, giving him a faintly outlaw look that she found very appealing. "There's more to it than that."

Once again, he'd seen things others had missed.

Susie's emotions bubbled to the surface. "I did it for Emmaline."

"I don't understand."

"When you're sick like I was, and Emmaline is now, all you want to do is get things back to normal as soon as possible. Any reminder—like the loss of your hair due to chemotherapy—gets in the way of that and makes you feel bad about yourself and the whole process of recovery. I spent far too much time during my illness resenting the loss of my hair and the way I looked, just as Emmaline is doing now. I think I would have been happier and gotten better sooner if I'd stopped resenting the changes in my appearance and instead embraced the opportunity to make over my image by adapting a different look. So I cut my hair in an attempt to show Emmaline that short hair is in vogue, and change is good. End of story."

"And I suppose it's coincidence that it's the same style as the wigs," he countered.

Susie tilted her head and regarded him meditatively. The thought of Tyler being so desperate to protect and understand her made her happy and she shrugged. "Sort of yes, sort of not."

"Why are you having them fixed up?" he

probed, giving her a look that told her this was only the warm-up to what he really wanted to ask.

Susie pretended an insouciance she couldn't begin to feel. "None of your business," she countered playfully, mocking his tone, which was far too serious for this early in the morning.

"Are the wigs for Emmaline?"

She blew out a breath before answering. "Yes, of course they are."

He regarded her stoically. "I just needed to make sure you hadn't come here to get some kind of treatment or second opinion."

"I don't need a first one!"

He moved as if to take her in his arms. "Susie—" His voice was soft, comforting.

She held up a hand. She wanted a lot of things from Tyler McCabe. Companionship, friendship, passion. She did not want pity or concern. "I can see you've done a lot of deducing, Sherlock," she told him drily, "but you've added two and two together and come up with five." She gave him a moment to absorb that. "I am not here because I have cancer or think I have cancer again. I am here because it's been a long time since I've done anything really nice for myself, and I thought I had earned a few days in a deluxe hotel."

"Is that the only reason you came to Dallas?"

"No." She had wanted to try and forget the humiliation of offering herself as his lover, only to be rejected. She had wanted to forget the hurt. The embarrassment. The crushing disappointment.

"Are you going to tell me what it is?" he pleaded softly, edging closer.

Of no mind to cooperate, Susie said, "Look around. Figure it out for yourself."

For the first time he seemed to notice the bags she had stacked against one wall. "You've been shopping."

"Brilliant."

"For Christmas presents?"

Trying not to think how much she liked the masculine fragrance of his soap and cologne, Susie tilted her head back. "As well as some new clothes for me. I figure if I'm going to be dating again, I should get some new duds."

He looked at her in silent reproach. "You sound happy about that."

"I figure if I'm going to do it, I might as well give it my all," Susie declared with a great deal more enthusiasm than she felt. "Who knows, maybe Bachelors Number Four or Five will be the one, and if not, maybe Number Six or Seven or Ten will be." Anything to keep her mind off Tyler and what they might have had if he'd only been amenable to the proposal she'd made.

"You're going to keep seeing the guys your parents fix you up with?" The set of his lips was grim.

"Why not?" She hated the fact that he looked so at peace with his refusal to sleep with her again when she was still tied up in knots. "Just because I don't see myself getting married or having kids doesn't mean I have to go through the rest of my life without love and sex. I'm sure if I put my heart and soul into looking I'll find someone who will happily meet my terms."

Unlike you, Tyler McCabe, she added silently, still feeling more than a little disappointed about his rejection of her, however well-meant.

Tyler inhaled deeply, shook his head. "You don't have to do that."

Susie smirked. She resented his interference, the way he was trying to impose restrictions on her life. "Really," she said sarcastically. Ignoring the flare of his nostrils and the set of his broad shoulders, she folded her arms in front of her and glared up at him. "You've decided that for me?"

He nodded. "I've had a change of heart, too," he said, the emotion in his low, husky voice countered by the studied casualness of his words. "I'm willing to adhere to your rules, Suze. Starting now, I'll be your lover and your friend."

Chapter Seven

Life is not a dress rehearsal.

"Thanks but no thanks,"

For the second time in twenty-four hours, Tyler was sure he hadn't heard her right. "Excuse me?"

"We had this discussion already," Susie muttered impatiently. She paced a safe distance away from him, obviously angry. "I don't want to go through it again."

She must have thought they were finished talking about it. He had plenty more to say. And he figured if she were honest, she did, too.

"I told you," he said slowly, pausing long enough to let his words sink in, "I changed my mind."

"So did I." Susie put up a staying hand. She had left her cardigan open, and he could see the silky bare skin of her stomach and the indentation of her navel above the low-slung pink-and-yellow-and-white-striped pajama pants. The soft curves of her breasts pushed against the stretchy cotton tank. She looked so sweet and enticing it was all he could do not to take her in his arms and worry about working out everything else later.

Not that she would have agreed to that. The feisty look in her eyes, and the lecturing quality of her voice told him as much.

Susie stepped closer, her bare feet looking impossibly dainty and feminine, right down to the pale pink polish on her toes.

Glaring up at him, she tossed her head, her short silky blond curls flying in every direction. "I don't need you to rush in and rescue me again just because you've concluded—" she tapped his chest with her index finger "—erroneously, I might add, that I am battling rogue cells again. And I certainly—" she tapped even harder "—don't need pity sex and or conditional friendship from you." She dropped her hand, stepped back. "So you're off the hook, Tyler McCabe. Just like with Catastrophe. You don't have to worry about me. I've found a safe haven for myself emotionally now. I know what I want." She began to pace, digging into the carpet with every step. "I know my parents—and believe me this chokes me to say it— are right." She gestured broadly, the action lifting her breasts. "I have been wasting a huge part of my life, only allowing myself a future when it comes to my work." Deliberately, she dropped her arms back to her sides. With her chin up, she stared deep into his eyes. "I deserve a whole life. I deserve love and passion and a lot more fun than I've been having the last ten years." She swallowed hard. "So I'm going to go out and get it."

Tyler moved closer. "That's great," he told her, genuinely happy to hear it. He had wanted this for her for a long time.

She regarded him with stony displeasure. "So you can leave."

This, he hadn't wanted. Tyler blinked. "You're kicking me out?"

Susie smiled tightly and continued holding his gaze. "It would appear so."

Tyler had been brought up a Texas gentleman. Therefore, he had to honor her wishes in this regard.

"Fine," he said reluctantly. "I'll go." He stepped to the side, cutting her off before she could show him the hotel room door. It was his turn to hold up a cautioning hand. "But not before I set the record straight." When she stopped dead in her tracks, he gently cupped her shoulders with his hands. "What I want from you, Suze, what I am prepared to give," he told her tenderly, "is about as far from pity sex as we can get."

She wanted to believe it. He could see it in her eyes. She just…didn't.

"Then what's it about?" Susie asked.

Tyler let his open palms drift down her arms, past her wrists, to her hands. "The road not taken," he explained gently, using up about the only poetry he could remember, but it was all too relevant nevertheless. "All the chances we've had and missed." Seeing he had her attention now, he tipped her chin up to his. "I want to see what we could have, Suze, if we let ourselves."

Intrigue flickered in her eyes, then extinguished, as suddenly as it had appeared. Once again, Tyler noted in dismay, her guard was up, more solidly in place than he had ever seen it.

Desperate to make her his, he promised, "Whatever your terms, I'll meet them."

Susie wet her lips with her tongue. "You're saying when it comes to the two of us I can have whatever I want from you, whenever I want it?"

Tyler conceded, "Absolutely."

Silence stretched between them, more intimate than ever before.

After a moment, Susie walked to the door and held it open. "I'll think about it and let you know."

"THE MESSAGE LIGHT ON YOUR answering machine is blinking," Eric Linden told Susie several days later, when he arrived to pick her up for their date.

Susie scrolled through the caller history list. Tyler, Tyler, Tyler. Like clockwork, he had called her three times a day since he'd left her hotel room in Dallas. Which made eight calls total now. She hadn't returned a one. Hadn't listened to them, either, for fear that if she did she would relent and end up seeing him again and wanting him in her bed.

She was afraid the two of them would start something with all the right intentions, only to have it end badly. She didn't think she could bear it to have him and then have him disappear on her again. She didn't care how noble or practical he thought he was being. It had hurt every time they had drifted close then drifted apart. Those feelings had forced her to put her guard up again, kept her from living the way she should have been living. But no more.

She was ready to embrace life again, and Eric Linden, outdoorsman and golf course architect extraordinaire, could be the one.

Bachelor Number Four certainly was cute enough to hold her attention. Blond, blue-eyed, handsome in sort of a Scandinavian way.

Her parents had chosen wisely this time.

So what if she didn't feel that jolt of sexual attraction she felt whenever Tyler was near? Those kind of sparks had proven not to be good for her. Instead, they disrupted the equilibrium of her life and heart.

Eric Linden appeared concerned about Susie's distracted state.

"If you want me to step outside on the porch while you listen to your messages, I'd be happy to do so."

"Thanks but this is nothing that can't wait."

She'd made a vow to move on without Tyler, at least for now, and she planned to keep it.

Susie smiled and grabbed her purse and keys. The November day was warm enough to leave her jacket behind.

She and Eric walked out to his low-slung sports car.

In keeping with her new attitude, Susie had decided to make this a real date. Hence, she'd let Eric decide the specifics. He was taking her out to the site of the new Laramie County Parks and Recreation Community Golf Course.

While Eric drove, he explained the basic layout of the design and the surveying that was currently going on.

Susie listened. Or tried to listen. She wasn't a golf fanatic, so many of the intricacies were lost on her. When they turned into the site and parked next to a host of other construction worker vehicles, she asked, "How long will you be in town?"

Eric held her door and because the seat was so low to the ground, assisted her out of the vehicle.

"I'll be staying in Laramie for the next six months or so, until all eighteen holes are completed and the course locker rooms and restaurant are built. Then I'll be on to my next job, which is in Central Florida."

"So you move around a lot." Susie fell into step beside Eric, her long skirt swishing around her calves.

Eric nodded. "As you can imagine, that makes it kind of hard. A lot of women don't want to get involved with someone with such a transient lifestyle." Then he paused and watched as her eyes followed a very familiar pickup truck turning into the makeshift parking area on the grass.

Susie's heart did a cartwheel in her chest.

She felt the blood drain from her face, then come back in a rush.

Eric looked at Susie. "Do you know him?"

She only wished she didn't. Ignoring the flush heating her cheeks, Susie nodded reluctantly.

Looking as though he owned the place, Tyler strode toward them, a welcoming grin on his face. "Hi, Suze." He winked at her sexily before turning to her date. "You must be Eric Linden. I'm Tyler McCabe."

Eric shook Tyler's hand. Eric frowned, perplexed. "That name is familiar."

Tyler wasn't surprised. "I'm on the Citizen's

Planning Board. We were instrumental in getting Laramie County to appropriate the funds for the course you're designing."

Eric snapped his fingers. "Of course. That's where I read your name. Did you come out here to witness the surveying of the property?" he asked cheerfully.

"Actually," Susie interrupted, deciding to end this little game here and now, "I think Tyler is here to annoy me."

Tyler gave her a rakish grin. He kept his eyes locked with hers as he allowed casually, "Susie's a little peeved at me right now."

"With very good reason, I might add," Susie interrupted, aiming a lethal look Tyler's way.

Tyler shrugged his broad shoulders and turned to Eric, man-to-man. "Sadly, she does not approve of my unflagging interest in local gossip. You know. Who's dating whom. Who slept with whom. Who's leaving whom."

"Guys talk about that kind of stuff here?" Eric looked amazed.

The corners of Tyler's mouth twitched. "Oh yeah. Incessantly. It's a small town. There's not much to do except discuss other people's private lives in great detail. Of course a lot of that is boring. Who wants to know that the Nedermeyers argued over whether or not to have chicken fried steak or chicken fried chicken for dinner. But occasionally, something really—" here Tyler whistled "—happens and some irate father takes off after his daughter's lover with a loaded shotgun and a pack of dogs, and well, let's just say, that can get pretty exciting."

Abruptly, Eric Linden's face was as pale as his white silk shirt. "The sheriff doesn't step in?"

"Eventually, sure," Tyler confirmed with an insufferable grin. "But first they've got to hear about it and get there and by then, well, usually all the real fireworks are over, and it's just about cleaning up the mess."

Eric looked a little green around the gills. "I need to talk to the surveyor. I'll be right back." He hurried off, his expensive loafers sinking in the tall grass.

Susie slammed her hands on her hips. She had feared all along that Tyler would not cease and desist when it came to interrupting and or ruining her dates. Steeling herself to take all the orneriness Tyler McCabe could dish out—and right now he appeared prepared to dish out plenty— she said through gritted teeth, "You can wipe that self-satisfied smirk off your face right now, Tyler McCabe."

Tyler tipped back the brim of his black hat so she could better see his eyes. "Gotta hand it to your folks," he pointed out sagely. "Bachelor Number Four is hot."

It was all Susie could do not to roll her eyes. "He's nice, Tyler," she corrected, color flowing into her cheeks.

Tyler ran a hand across his jaw. "A mite skittish, in my opinion. But then what do I know, I'm just a dumb, unsophisticated country boy."

She batted her eyelashes at him flirtatiously. "Who's as full of beans as can be."

"Actually, I had a fajita salad for lunch, if you must know."

Susie stiffened. His arrogance was infuriating! "I thought you were going to stop interfering with my dates!"

He stepped so close she had to tilt her head back to see his face. "Suze, I haven't begun to interfere with your dates."

Susie resisted the urge to run before they ended up doing something reckless and foolish, like kissing again. She held his gaze defiantly. "It's not going to do you any good."

"That remains to be seen. I think I just cleared the playing field a little bit."

"Exactly my point," Susie said with indignance. "This isn't a game, Tyler."

He arched his brow. A sense of purpose glittered in his hazel eyes. "If it weren't, you'd give me a fighting chance."

Susie's heart gave a nervous kick against her ribs. "Give me one good reason why I should!" she demanded.

"Because—" Tyler stepped forward, took her in his arms and kissed her soundly on the lips before slowly lifting his head once again "—you owe me at least that much."

"I most certainly do n—"

Susie's protest was cut off by a second, searing kiss. And unlike the first, this one did not come to a swift end.

Tyler knew she didn't mean to be kissing him back, any more than he meant to be kissing her here and now. And somehow that made the culmination of their mutual desire all the more pleasing. Groaning, he drew her ever closer, so her breasts were flattened against the hard wall of his chest, her lower half pressed against his. He felt her tremble, and shudder. He deepened the kiss all the more, exploring her soft, sweet mouth and the play of her lips against his. Never passive, she took the lead, kissing him back, wreathing her hands through his hair.

And it was then that they heard the discreet cough behind them.

Reluctantly, Tyler let her go.

Susie turned to her date, her face hot with embarrassment.

Eric Linden stood there, waiting. He looked more annoyed than jealous. "Something I should know about you two?"

Tyler had an inkling how the other man felt. It was always a pain to realize you were wasting your time.

"Yes," he said, figuring the guy deserved to know where he stood with Susie, which was nowhere, at least as long as Tyler was in the picture, and he intended to stay in the picture. "If you want a chance at this gal's heart," he told Eric, "you better get your track shoes on."

Susie glared at Tyler and stepped away from both men. She smiled at Tyler sweetly. "I guess that means you're out of the running, Tyler McCabe," she said, pointing at his feet, "because you're wearing cowboy boots."

"See what I mean?" Tyler said to Eric with a disparaging shake of his head. "She encourages this kind of rivalry."

Susie's mouth fell open. "I do not!"

Tyler scoffed, playing the moment for all it was worth. He closed the distance between them, not stopping until he towered over her once again. "Then tell Eric here how many men you have vowed to date," he commanded.

Susie clamped her jaw shut, glared up at Tyler. "That was a private argument, Tyler."

"See?" Tyler turned back to Susie's date, hands spread wide. "She's afraid to tell you, Eric."

Susie tossed her head. "I am not!"

Tyler enjoyed the sight of her, so pretty and mussed in that just-been-kissed way. In the way that said that soon she would be his. And not just temporarily or as the result of some crisis this time. "Then?" he prodded.

Susie harrumphed. "I said I would date as many guys as possible until I found someone I could be happy with."

"The way she's going, she could reject hundreds of guys who just aren't right. And in the meantime, she'll keep stringing along the guys like me who've been around forever."

"I don't know what is going on between the two of you but it is clear that something is, so Susie, lovely as it was to meet you, our date is over."

"Does that mean I can take her home?" Tyler asked, glad Eric had been so quick to see the light.

Scowling, Eric waved his hand as if showing them both the exit. "Be my guest." Eric strode back down the hill to the surveyor.

Tyler turned back to the woman who was now his date. "You going to ride with me? Or walk?" Tyler asked.

Susie aimed a lethal look his way. "Oh, you're driving me home, all right. And that is the last place you are ever going to drive me!"

"THIS ISN'T THE WAY BACK to town," Susie observed, minutes later.

"I have to stop by Healing Meadow first, to check on Catastrophe."

Forgetting for a moment her hurry to distance herself from Tyler, Susie asked, "How's the horse doing?"

Tyler's expression turned serious. "We're still watching for signs of complications, but so far there are none."

Susie exhaled in relief. "Poor thing. I can't imagine what it's like to be suspended like that."

Tyler shrugged. "It's not the most comfortable position in the world, but we're giving him medicine to keep him as relaxed and calm as possible."

Minutes later, when they entered the hospital barn and walked down to the stall where Catastrophe was being treated, Susie couldn't help but admire the big stallion with the glossy brown coat and silky black mane and tail. Catastrophe was still in the harness that kept the weight off his healing leg but the horse looked straight at Susie and Tyler, lifting his tail, circling his head, and nickering softly. All positive signs, she knew.

Tyler talked gently to the horse, as he examined

him, then patted him affectionately and gave him a slice of apple.

Watching, Susie smiled. There was no doubt about it. Tyler had a magic touch for animals and humans alike. "How is his injured leg?" she asked.

"It's healing nicely. Complications can still develop, but so far, so good." Tyler cut another piece of apple for Catastrophe and handed it to Susie.

Susie offered it to the stallion. "He's lucky he had you," she murmured to Tyler. "Otherwise..."

"He'd be history," Tyler guessed what Susie was about to say.

Susie nodded. "Right."

Tyler paused to speak to the vet tech, then he and Susie walked out of the hospital barn. Too late, Susie realized she had let her guard down once again. Unwise, given the fact that Tyler was who he was, take it or leave it. And what they had offered each other in the past had not been nearly enough. She wanted to move on, she wanted to expand her hopes for the future, without getting her heart broken once again. She didn't want to be the prize in a testosterone-driven competition. She didn't want to be rescued or comforted. She wasn't even sure she wanted to be desired for mutual physical pleasure or turned into a friend with benefits. What had sounded intellectually sophisticated and physically practical at the outset, no longer seemed so simple. She was beginning to see she couldn't rein in her emotions any more than she could shut them down entirely. Tyler McCabe had the capacity to break her heart. And then some. And that alone was a risk Susie didn't want to take.

Tyler inclined his head to the side. "I have to go inside the house for a minute and check my messages." His gaze roved her face with leisurely appreciation. "Want to come?"

"No."

"Suit yourself," Tyler said with a grin, "but I'm fairly sure there's an ice-cold root beer with your name on it in there."

Susie thought about standing outside. Then decided what the heck. She had a few things she wanted to say to the big lug in any case.

She followed him inside to his study and watched as he sat down on a corner of his desk and got right to work.

Deciding a cold drink wasn't such a bad idea while she was killing time, she wandered into his sparsely outfitted kitchen and helped herself to a bottle of her favorite root beer from the fridge. It was gone by the time Tyler was finished talking.

She lounged in the doorway of his study, trying not to think how relaxed he looked in the oak-paneled lair, with the massive desk, state-of-the-art computer and filled bookshelves.

Whereas it took every ounce of self-control she had to remain where she was and appear unaffected by his masculine presence and her latent desire. "You can't keep doing this," she said.

"Check my messages or return calls to my patients' owners?" he asked, putting the cordless phone back on the base.

"Harass me."

Tyler leaned back and clamped his arms over his broad chest. "I'm not harassing you."

"Then what do you call it?"

"Pursuing you."

Susie gulped. "Why?"

"Because I want my chance," Tyler countered, challenging her all the more. He stepped closer, his body exuding so much heat it felt like Texas in July.

Susie pivoted away from him. "It could be argued that you already had your chance." She stood so his desk was between them.

His expression intent, he kept his eyes locked with hers. "That was before I had my change of heart."

Suddenly, Susie was trembling. "Why should I trust your change of heart?"

He came closer, tenderness and compassion on

his face. "Because to do otherwise would leave you always wondering what you were missing and what might have been," he told her softly.

"Talk about ego!" Susie shot back, squaring her shoulders, and retaining her calm despite the glimmer of mischief in his beautiful eyes.

"It's not ego," he told her gruffly, catching her wrist before she could walk away again. "It's fact. You desire me." Tyler clamped one arm around her waist, threaded the other hand through her hair and brought her against him, length to length. "I desire you. It's always been that way, and probably always will." He gazed down at her, all determined male. "We just haven't allowed ourselves to act on that desire very often."

"Which was probably smart of both of us," she countered, her throat so dry she could hardly swallow.

A gentle smile tugged at the corners of his lips. He shifted her up onto the desk in his study and trapped her between his spread legs. "Or very, very dumb."

Susie's heart began to pound. "Tyler…"

He flattened his hands on either side of her and leaned in close, cosseting her with warmth. "Here's the thing, Suze. I don't want you to be ticked off at me."

She tried to move his arms so she could escape.

It was like trying to budge a one-hundred-year-old oak, so she quit trying and angled her head at him instead. Worse than his happy smile was the look of satisfaction on his face. She brought her hands up through the narrow space between their bodies and splayed them across his chest. "Too late."

He gave her a look that reminded her that he knew her better than anyone, even when she would have preferred he not.

Ignoring her waning resistance, he bent to kiss her throat, tracing a lazy circle where her pulse throbbed. "And since the only reason you are peeved at me is because I didn't make love to you when I had the chance, there's only one way to fix it. And that's make love to you now."

He took her all the way in his arms and captured her mouth in a soft kiss that had her senses spinning and her heart soaring.

"This won't change anything," Susie protested, even when she tilted her head to give him deeper access.

The possessive look in his eyes robbed her of the will to resist. "We'll see about that."

He kissed her, holding nothing back. Without breaking the kiss, he guided her off the desk and danced her backward, through his house, to his bed. Half a dozen times, Susie meant to call a halt but he was so warm and solid and real. He was here, and so was she. And the moment lent a much-needed romance to her often stark world.

Savoring his strength and the safe harbor of his arms, she allowed him to kiss her and kiss her until passion swept through her, her body arched and her hands clung.

Her pulse jumped as he pressed light kisses across the nape of her neck, to the V of her sweater.

She lost what was left of her restraint. A soft moan—or was it a sigh of surrender?—shuddered through her. Already feeling the dampness between her legs, and the desire pounding through her, she let him undress her, and lay her back on the covers of his bed.

He gave her a look that promised this evening would be every bit as memorable as she wanted it to be. "When you look at me like that...all sweet and womanly...it drives me wild," he murmured, kissing her again and again until her heart beat in urgent rhythm to his.

"Oh, Tyler," Susie whispered. The two of them had made love before, but she had never experienced anything like this intense aching need. She had never wanted him quite so recklessly. Never wanted him with all her heart and soul, the way she did right now. The way, his glance said, he wanted her, too.

She watched with a mixture of wonder and appreciation as he undressed. The soft light of the bedroom illuminated the hard ridges and taut planes of his body. His shoulders were broad and strong. Satiny skin and a mat of reddish-brown hair covered his well-defined pecs and narrowed down to a flat abdomen.

As the last of his clothing fell to the floor, and he joined her on the bed, she couldn't contain a low sound of appreciation.

She pressed a kiss on his collarbone, shoulder, jaw. "I don't know why I can't resist you."

Amusement twinkled in his eyes. He twined a lock of her hair around his fingertip, and stared deep into her eyes. "Yes," he countered softly, meaningfully. "You do. It's the same reason I can't resist you."

He kissed her gently, his tongue mating with hers, his lower half pressed erotically against hers. Engulfing her with the heat and strength of his body, he continued kissing her until Susie's whole body was alive, quivering with urgent sensations. Susie felt so many things. Cherished. Adored. Wanted. Needed. She felt alive in a way she hadn't ever experienced. She moaned as his hands swept down her body, molding and exploring. She arched against him, yearning for a more intimate union. And then his lips moved even lower, to the curves and slope and jutting tips of her breasts. Desire trembled inside her, making her belly feel weightless, soft. She yielded to his every kiss and caress, burying her hands in his hair as he sent her into a frenzy of wanting. She could feel his erection, hot and urgent, pressing against her, his heart pounding in his chest. They were practically combusting, and they'd barely gotten started.

He slid down her body, stroking the hollow of her stomach, kissing the nest of golden curls. And then he was nudging her thighs apart with his knee, settling between her legs, sliding ever lower. What few boundaries that existed between them dissolved. Susie threw back her head and gripped his shoulders hard, arching up to meet him as he claimed her, touching and kissing her languidly, taking her to heights and depths, exploring every nuance of desire, until there was no doubt he'd completely rocked her world, no doubt how much she needed him, and he her. Only when her response had gentled once again, did he shift upward, pulling her knees to his waist.

"That's it," he whispered as she opened herself up to him, and their bodies melded in boneless pleasure. "Take me. Take all of me."

For a moment, Susie didn't think it was going to be possible, not when he was this aroused. But as he slid his arm beneath her and lifted her against him, they slipped into a union that was wonderfully sensual, hot and wild. He caught her by the hips, letting her do for him, with the most feminine part of her, what he had already done for her. Murmuring her name between sweet, sipping kisses, he took his time, possessing her with tantalizing slowness, going ever deeper, harder, slower, even as he demanded she surrender to him completely.

The mixture of tenderness, passion, pleasure, left her feeling deliciously distraught. Their eyes locked. Their lips met. He pressed into her as deeply as he could go. She lifted her hips and offered him refuge, knowing even as they neared completion that it wasn't enough, that there could be more.

Holding him tighter, she kissed him more and more deeply, surrendering to his every move, his every wish, until there was no more prolonging the inevitable and the two of them went spiraling over the edge. And then they were lost in an explosion of lust and feeling unlike anything Susie had ever known.

Long moments passed as they clung to each other breathlessly, in awe at the abandon they had shown. Susie's body tingled with satisfaction, but, not all that surprisingly, by the time she caught her breath, her heart and mind were once again in turmoil.

Too late, Susie realized that they'd been fools to think they could contain this to a "friends who had sex" situation.

She didn't know how Tyler felt. Except that he desired her as no man ever had or possibly ever would. And while that might be fine for him, the truth was, she could fall in love with Tyler. Not the kind of safe, emotionally distant type of relationship that she yearned for, but the I-can't-bear-to-be-without-him love that she had always feared.

Needing someone that way scared the hell out of her.

It made her wonder what would happen if her luck ran out and her illness returned.

It made her think that she might hurt Tyler by putting him through the kind of hell she had already experienced. And that was the last thing she had ever wanted.

The last thing he deserved.

Trembling, she extricated herself from his arms. She tried not to think how easy it would be to get used to this. "I have to go." Hurriedly, she snatched up her clothes and began to dress.

Tyler sat up, the sheet falling to his waist, an inscrutable look on his handsome face.

"Stay the night," he urged her quietly, persuasively, looking deep into her eyes.

Susie met his glance and knew her heart was in even deeper jeopardy.

She swallowed hard and put up a hand to stave off further talk about it. "I can't." She inhaled a bolstering breath. What she was doing was best for both of them. "Please, Tyler, take me home." She thrust her hands into the pockets of her jacket to still their trembling and looked him square in the eye. "Take me home right now."

TYLER KNEW IT HAD BEEN a mistake to make love to Susie tonight, and that notion had been confirmed the moment she pulled away from him as soon as their passion was spent.

She hadn't been ready for it, despite her protestations to the contrary. Unfortunately, it was a little too late to unring that bell now. They'd just have to make do.

And they'd start with a heart-to-heart.

Figuring a little time to pull herself together emotionally would be helpful, Tyler waited until their commandeered "date" was over and he had walked Susie up on her front porch.

"I'm not letting you go until we talk."

Cheeks still flushed from their lovemaking, Susie ran a hand through her tousled curls. "I think we've demonstrated that talking gets us in trouble. As does just about everything else we do together on an ordinary, noncrisis basis."

Tyler rested a shoulder against the porch post. He had no problem hearing her out, even if what she had to say wasn't what he wanted to hear, or thought. He lifted a brow. "You're saying you want us to go back to being buddies?"

Susie bit her lower lip. "Yes. No. I don't know." She threw up her hands and began to pace, her boots clacking across the wooden porch. "But you were right about one thing," she said firmly. "I was mad at you for not making love to me when I suggested we become lovers." Regret colored her expression. "And that's not fair," she admitted with a soft, telling shake of her head. "You were just telling me how you felt. I should have accepted it. Let it be."

Finished being an observer in this drama of wills, Tyler closed the distance between them and took her by the shoulders. "It's not possible for us to do that anymore, Suze." He caressed the curve of her cheek, felt the heat of her skin beneath his palm. "We can't go back to what we were. All we can do is move forward."

Susie splayed both hands across his chest, and pushed away from him. "To what?" she said.

Tyler let his hands fall back to his sides. "To whatever you want. You can set the terms," he added. "Just don't shut me out. Don't run away from me again."

Instead of being reassured, as he had hoped, Susie looked all the more distraught. "I need to think."

Tyler exhaled. "Okay."

She glared at him. "And I have to go on a date with Bachelor Number Five that I would really appreciate you not crashing. It's not fair to the other guy," she mumbled.

"And it embarrasses you," Tyler added, trying not to think how cute she was when she was angry with him.

Susie rolled her eyes. "Gee. You think?"

Tyler grinned. The return of her sassy sarcasm could only be a good sign. "All right," he conceded reluctantly. "I'll let your date with Bachelor Number Five happen exactly as it is supposed to unfold." He paused, thinking. "Do you know who he is?"

Susie shook her head, her hand already on the doorknob. "My parents haven't told me yet. I'll have to call them to find out."

Tyler nodded grimly. "Just do me a favor," he instructed, "and get it over with quickly."

Chapter Eight

If you're headed in the right direction, each step, no matter how small, gets you closer to your goal.

"I thought Tyler McCabe was going to help you with this," Meg said as she sat in her dining room, cutting lengths of orange, brown and gold ribbon.

Susie set up stacks of pages for the Thanksgiving gratitude journals on the marble-topped buffet against the opposite wall. She tried not to think how many "projects" she and Meg had done together over the years. Or what her childhood would have been like had her father not married Meg several years after her own mother died.

Susie shrugged and pushed away her uncharacteristic uncertainty. "I changed my mind."

Clearly aware how unlike Susie this was, Meg lifted a brow. "And decided to have Bachelor Number Five do it with you instead?"

Susie pretended she wouldn't rather be sitting

somewhere with Tyler right now. "I figured it would be a good test of character," she fibbed. "If Ernest Pierce is willing to help me out with something this laborious on our first date, he can't be all bad."

"Oh, he was willing all right." Finished with the first rolls of ribbon, Meg got three more out of the fabric store bag. "But back to Tyler. What is going on between the two of you?"

Susie avoided looking directly into Meg's eyes. "What makes you think anything is going on?"

Meg smiled. "Chalk it up to mother's intuition."

Susie took a page from each stack, ran a length of ribbon through the prepunched holes in the paper and secured the journal with a bow, all without saying a word.

"It might help you to confide in someone," Meg said after a moment.

Susie supposed that was true enough. She released a frustrated breath and pushed a hand through her hair. "He wants us to be friends."

Meg frowned. "I thought you were."

"He means all the time, not just when one of us has got some sort of misery going on in our lives," Susie explained.

Meg sat back in her chair. "And that's a problem?"

It was if she fell in love with him.

"I'm attracted to him," Susie said with another sigh.

Meg scoffed and continued cutting ribbon. "Who doesn't know that?"

Susie's hands stilled. "What do you mean?"

Meg gave her an indulgent smile. "Honey, every time you look at him… Even your father can see the emotional intimacy between you and Tyler. And your father tries not to see those kinds of things when it comes to his daughters, if you know what I mean."

She certainly did. Susie relaxed. "Dad can be a tad overprotective."

Meg chuckled. "Just a tad?"

"Okay, a lot." Which was why she couldn't let on that she and Tyler had made love again.

Neither Meg nor Luke would approve of her having recreational sex with no strings attached. And yet, how could she regret something that had felt so good, that had made her feel so warm and wanted and alive?

Meg narrowed her gaze. "Has Tyler been putting the moves on you?"

Susie flushed and went back to arranging pages in the right order. "Why would you think that?" She tried to sound calm.

"Maybe Tyler wants your relationship to change."

I know he does.

"I'm not sure that's a good idea." Susie looked down and willed her fingers to stop trembling. "It's helped me, knowing that he is always there for me in a crisis." She bit her lip. "If we were to pursue something else, and then one of us changed our mind or it didn't work out the way we hoped and planned, things could get very awkward, very fast."

Meg nodded with understanding. "On the other hand, if you don't allow yourself the freedom to see where your relationship with Tyler could go, you could be missing out on something really terrific."

Which was, Susie thought ruefully, precisely the dilemma she had been wrestling with since last night.

Unfortunately, despite the passage of time and much consideration, she was no closer to knowing what to do.

She only knew the thought of not making love with Tyler again very soon left her feeling very blue.

The doorbell rang. Relieved to have this heart-to-heart cut short before Meg discovered anything else, Susie looked at her watch. "Good ol' Ernie Pierce is five minutes early."

Meg smiled in approval. "That must mean he is eager to start your date."

Susie sighed. If only she were half as enthusiastic. But how could she be when all she was thinking about was the way Tyler's body had felt next to hers? They weren't committed to each other, yet here she was, feeling guilty and disloyal as all-get-out…almost as if she were cheating on Tyler, just meeting with the other guy.

"You want me to get that?" Meg asked, when Susie still hadn't moved, and the doorbell rang again.

Susie gave her a tentative smile. "If you wouldn't mind, that would be great."

Meg disappeared. Susie heard the front door open, then close. But curiously, no words were spoken. None that she could hear anyway.

Two sets of footsteps came closer. Susie turned as Meg and guest approached the dining room entryway.

When she saw who was standing there, her jaw dropped.

"I'll leave you two alone," Meg said and beat a hasty retreat.

Tyler leaned casually against the door frame. He was dressed in nice jeans and a black Western shirt. He looked at her as if he had come to claim her. "Aren't you going to invite me in?"

His conceit was outrageous. Susie pushed back her chair and stood. "I can't believe you." Her heart skipped a beat as she approached him. "You have to go."

Fine lines appeared at the corners of his eyes and he laughed. "Why?"

Susie stiffened in indignation. "Because as you very well know I am expecting Bachelor Number Five any minute!" Then added, "Which is obviously why you're here."

To Susie's further frustration, Tyler didn't even bother to deny it.

Tyler strolled on in as though he owned the place. "Maybe Bachelor Number Five won't mind if I join you."

"Oh. Please." Susie's knees trembled as she waved Tyler away. "I don't know much about Ernie Pierce except that he is a self-made man, and a good sport, to boot. But there's no way he is going to want another man chaperoning his first date with me."

Tyler stopped just short of her. He rubbed a hand across his jaw. "You're probably right about that." He dropped his hand to his side and lowered his face to hers. "Us guys do tend to get territorial about the women we are interested in."

Susie flushed self-consciously. "Then you understand why you have to leave."

"To make way for the new guy," he said, lazily taking in her black jeans and black turtleneck sweater.

Susie nodded, wishing he weren't so much taller than she was. Even with two-inch-heeled boots on, Tyler dwarfed her by a good six inches. "Right."

Half his mouth crooked up in a taunting smile. "Only one thing."

Susie planted her hands on her hips. "And what is that?" she demanded impatiently.

Tyler angled his thumb at the center of his chest. "I'm Ernie Pierce."

TYLER HAD BEEN WAITING FOR her reaction to his ploy. It wasn't long in coming. Her soft lips pursed in a way that had him wanting to kiss her all over again. Her eyes were full of amber fire. Tossing her head so her curls bounced against her face, she scoffed, "You don't really expect me to believe that."

"Actually, I do."

"Yeah, well, likely story."

Tyler tried to look innocent. He didn't know why he liked getting under her skin so much. He just did.

Aware she was still waiting for an explanation, he placed a hand on his chest. "My full name is Tyler Ernest Pierce McCabe. My brothers Teddy and Trevor and I all kept our birth father's name when Travis adopted us. We just added the Mc-Cabe to the end."

Susie scowled. Beginning, he assumed, to believe...

Meg stuck her head in. She had a jacket on, her shoulder bag slung over her arm. She smiled at Susie. "Sweetheart, I'm off to meet your father for dinner and a movie. So have fun."

Susie gaped. "Mom!"

"Goodbye, dear." Meg turned to him. "And Tyler—good luck. I think you're going to need it." She disappeared.

Seconds later, the front door shut.

The two of them were quite definitely alone.

Susie continued glaring at him. "How did you get them to agree to this?"

It hadn't been easy. Tyler pulled out a chair and sat down. Anchoring her wrist, he tugged her down onto his lap. "I told your mom and dad that it wouldn't be fair to drag another guy into this whole dating thing when you were only going to turn him down eventually anyway."

"You don't know that."

"Yes. I do." Tyler cupped her face in his palm. "I want you to be my woman, Susie." Unable to help himself, he scored his thumb across her lips, tracing the delicate shape. "I thought I made that clear last night."

"Woman?" To his chagrin, she still looked confused and upset.

"Yes, woman," he repeated firmly, trying not to think how warm and taut and utterly feminine her body felt draped over his. "And I'm talking exclusive." He worked his hands down her spine.

Susie bit her lip and for the first time since he had walked in, averted her eyes. "Our parents aren't going to approve of this," she murmured, distraught.

Tyler blinked. "What are you talking about? They're going to love the fact that we're dating."

She scoffed and pushed to her feet. "With no plans to ever marry?" Hands cupping her elbows, she glided away. "I doubt it."

Wishing he had never made such a foolhardy agreement with her, Tyler followed. He clasped her shoulders, crowding her and forcing her to look at him again. "I think you underestimate them, Suze," he said softly. "Sure, our folks would rather see us hitched with a dozen kids around us, but if that's not in the cards, if that particular American Dream is not right for us, they're going to want us to find one that is. And they're going to want to know that you and I have someone in our lives to love and be loved by in return."

Susie's eyes glistened with emotion. She

smoothed a hand absently across his chest. "You've thought this out," she said sweetly.

To a point. "All I know is what's in here." He captured her hand and held it against the left side of his chest, over his heart. "And that's you, you, you...."

SUSIE HAD TIME TO EVADE Tyler's kiss if she wanted. But the moment he threaded his hand through the hair at the nape of her neck and tipped her face to his, she knew, ignoring the growing feelings between them was not what she wanted at all. She opened her lips to the pressure of his and returned his kiss deeply, passionately. He kissed her as if he meant to make her his, not just for now, but for all time. Yearning swept through her, overwhelming her heart and her mind. She wrapped her arms about his neck, drawing him closer yet, fitting her soft curves against the hard warmth of his chest. She loved the sexy, male scent of him. She loved the reckless, womanly way he made her feel, and she found herself needing and wanting Tyler the way she had never needed and wanted anyone. He was hard, too.

Both of them were trembling when he finally let her go.

All too aware they'd just been making out in her parents' dining room like a couple of teenagers with no place else to go, she stepped away from him, trembling.

He shot her a wry look, turning suddenly serious. "You ready to go?"

Ready to make love was more like it, Susie thought. But not here, and not now. She folded her arms in front of her, taking up the contentious stance she should have used much earlier. "I hate to break it to you, Tyler. But we still have two hundred and fifty gratitude journals to put together."

He waved off her concern. "I've got that covered," he said lazily.

She searched his face for clues as to what he was up to now. "You do?"

"Yep. Seems a group of the women are putting together the centerpieces for Thanksgiving dinner out at my parents' ranch tomorrow afternoon— they're using the testing center for Annie's Homemade products.

Susie had been there before. Located in a converted barn, the large cement-floored room resembled a cafeteria. Focus groups were invited to sit at the gingham-covered picnic tables and give their reaction to the latest barbecue sauces, condiments and fruit spreads made by the company Tyler's mom owned.

"I talked my mom into expanding tomorrow's activities to include the gratitude journal assembly. And I invited Emmaline, my two younger brothers and some of my cousins that are also high school age to help. I figured if Emmaline met some of the kids her age that are going to be at Thanksgiving dinner she'd be more excited about attending. Right now, I get the impression she's still dreading it."

"Good thinking."

"Plus it gets us off the hook tonight so we can go on our first date."

She'd known there was more. She narrowed her eyes. "Which is going to be..."

"A surprise." He flashed her a confident grin. "Good thing you're dressed in jeans and a sweater, though. It's getting a little cold out tonight. You might want to grab a jacket, too."

Susie had one with her. She went to the hall closet to get it. "What are we going to be doing?"

He held her suede coat while she slipped her arms into the sleeves. "I could tell you."

"But you won't."

Eyes glimmering mischievously, he said, "You'll find out soon enough."

Twenty minutes later, Tyler was turning his pickup truck into the drive of Healing Meadow Ranch. He parked next to the hospital barn, instead of the ranch house. "I hope you don't mind."

He cut the engine and withdrew the keys from the ignition. "I've got to check on Catastrophe first."

"No problem." Susie fell into step beside him as they walked toward the entrance. "How's he doing?"

Tyler slipped a protective hand behind her waist as they reached the door. "The antibiotics seem to be working on the infection."

Susie waited for him to open the door for her. "But you're not going to relax until the leg is entirely healed and he's walking again."

"Right."

Looking calm but alert, Catastrophe greeted Tyler with a nicker, dropping his head and then flipping it high, making a full skyward circle with his nose. He flicked his tail as Tyler stepped into the stall, and examined not only the leg around the cast, but the sling that kept Catastrophe immobilized.

Susie was amazed that the horse could seem so happy and content under the circumstances, and was pleased to know Catastrophe's life was the result of Tyler's intervention. She stayed on the other side of the stall door, gently running her hand down his mane, loving the silky texture. "He really is a beautiful animal."

Tyler nodded in agreement, wrote a few things

on the chart and handed it back to the vet tech on duty at the hospital barn for the night.

Susie could see that as much as Tyler cared about the animal, he had already distanced himself emotionally. His concern now was strictly veterinary.

That shouldn't have surprised her.

He had always been able to do the same thing with her. Come into her life when she needed him. Exit seamlessly when she no longer did.

Being able to step away when the time came was something Tyler was still very, very good at doing.

Susie did not have the same talent.

If she had been the one personally rescuing and then caring for Catastrophe, there was no way she would have been able to give the beautiful stallion away and emerge with her heart intact.

Wordlessly, Susie watched Tyler check on the other animals in the hospital barn. Another ailing horse, a baby calf and a mule. He used the same caring touch and attention to detail on all.

"It all looks good," Tyler said finally, returning to the vet tech on duty. He paused, concern on his face. "Any further word on Smokey?"

"None so far," the vet tech replied.

Tyler nodded. "If anything comes up, I'll have my pager on. Otherwise—" Tyler paused to give

Catastrophe a final rubdown on the neck and face "—you-all have a good night and I'll be by again in the morning."

"Will do, Doc," the vet tech said.

Together, Tyler and Susie left the barn.

Once again, their steps were perfectly meshed.

"I'm assuming Smokey is another one of your patients."

"You assume right."

Which meant it was none of her business. Unless he chose to talk about it, and he clearly did not. "So now what?" Susie asked, turning to her "date" for the evening, the ignominious Bachelor Number Five....

Tyler smiled, all barely leashed male energy once again. "We go on our very first snipe hunt."

SUSIE SCOFFED AND ROLLED her eyes. *Seriously. Seriously!* "There is no such thing as a snipe, Tyler McCabe."

Tyler lifted a challenging brow. He leaned closer, not stopping until they were cheek to cheek and nose to nose. "Have you ever seen one?"

Well... "No. I have not."

His hazel eyes twinkled mischievously. He lifted his broad shoulders in an aimless shrug. "Then how do you know?"

Susie held her ground and folded her arms in

front of her defiantly. "Because I wasn't born yesterday?" she teased.

Tyler paused to unlock the back door of the house, then led them into the mudroom. He used the toe of his boot to push aside a box heaped with old towels, and plucked two heavy-duty flashlights and an over-the-shoulder day pack with mesh panels sewn into the side off the washer.

"What's that for?" Susie asked.

To her irritation, Tyler's expression remained smug as he explained matter-of-factly, "The flashlights are so we can find the snipes, the day pack so we can carry them back if we find any."

Exasperated, Susie said, "You're really going to pursue this."

"With or without you," Tyler affirmed, pausing to look deep into her eyes, "but I was really hoping you would come with me."

"You're serious."

He mugged in all innocence. "Would I put you on?"

Susie stifled a laugh. "That's just it. I don't know."

He agreed in mock solemnity. "Precisely why we should be dating."

Susie rolled her eyes again. He chuckled. They headed out. Susie buttoned her jacket up against the cold night air.

Looking very intent on his task, Tyler led the way across his backyard, helped her climb a fence, then swung himself over after her. He flipped on his flashlight and headed out into the meadow of knee-high grass, scrub oak and cedar.

"You sure there are no snakes out here?" Susie asked, shivering at the thought.

"Nope. Which is why you should have your light on."

He didn't have to tell her twice. Susie turned on her flashlight. The powerful beam spread a wide arc as they moved quietly through the grass.

"So what does a 'snipe' look like?" she asked eventually, aware Tyler really did seem to be searching high and low for something in the dark Texas night. Which made her wonder if there wasn't a real animal also known as a snipe.

"Just keep a lookout for the whites of their eyes," Tyler advised.

If he was yanking her chain, he was doing a damn fine job of it. "You said their eyes? Plural?"

Tyler nodded, looking around the base of an oak tree. "Should be more than one when we find 'em, yeah."

Wind swept across the meadow, chill and damp. Clouds moved overhead, partially obscuring the stars and moon.

"Okay…"

Tyler paused abruptly, then slowly turned to face her. He narrowed his eyes. "Did you hear that?"

"What?"

"The rustling in the grass."

Susie stepped closer, making no effort to be quiet. "Don't you think you're taking this a little too far?"

"Shhh!" He leaned close. "You'll scare 'em away," he whispered in her ear.

Tingling from the warmth of his breath, Susie drew back and sighed. "If you say so."

He didn't smile.

Didn't move.

Every inch of Tyler was on high alert.

Ignoring her completely now, he stared into the darkness, moving the arc of his flashlight over the grass. Back and forth. Low, toward the ground.

Susie was about to make another smart remark when a jet black blur of fur zipped past before disappearing into the weeds.

"Was that a…" Susie frowned. It couldn't have been a raccoon or a skunk because whatever the animal had been, it was a solid color.

"Exactly what we're looking for," Tyler whispered back, firm hand on her arm. "You go that way." He aimed his flashlight to the left. "I'll go right. And be careful not to step on any nests."

"Right. Nests," Susie muttered, shivering more from the fear of unknown black furry critters now than the cold.

Tyler kept going. Stopped suddenly. He arced his light at her, shining it right in her eyes, before moving it away.

Susie looked at him.

He was motioning her toward him urgently.

As she neared, he put his finger to his lips indicating silence.

The expression on his face indicated he wasn't kidding.

As quietly as possible, Susie waded through the knee-high grass, taking the path he had already trampled. When she reached his side, she saw what all the fuss was about. And it was enough to simultaneously fill her with wonder and break her heart on this cold, damp, dark Texas night.

"Those aren't snipes," Susie whispered in awe, kneeling down beside him. "Those are newborn kittens."

"ABOUT TWENTY-FOUR HOURS old from the looks of it," Tyler said tenderly. He took the day pack off his shoulder and opened it up. Handing it to her, he put the four kittens gently in the bottom, one after another. A loud yowl followed, and then the mother cat hurled herself at him. He caught the mama cat around the middle and put the struggling animal in the sack with her kittens. Almost immediately, she settled down.

"This is what we were looking for," Susie guessed as she and Tyler headed back to the house.

Tyler zipped the top shut, cradled the knapsack in his arms, and headed back toward the ranch house at a much brisker clip.

"Yeah. Smokey—that's what we've been calling her—is a stray who showed up about a week ago, obviously very pregnant. We couldn't get her to come close enough to be able to pick her up, so we were leaving milk and kibble out for her. Then about two days ago, she stopped coming round altogether. I figured she went off somewhere quiet to have her kittens, but it's too cold for her to be keeping them out here now. Not to mention dangerous." At Susie's inquiring look, he said simply, "Predators. Anyway, I figured she might go off in search of her supper once the sun went down, which gave us a chance to find the nest. Turns out I was right."

They paused to hop the pasture fence once again.

"Why didn't you tell me what we were looking for?" Susie went first, then cradled the knapsack of trembling kittens and mama cat while he followed.

He offered an engaging half grin. "I wasn't sure we'd find them, although I hoped we would, and I didn't want you worrying. Second, I wanted our first date to be memorable." They reached the ranch house once again.

Tyler opened the door. He shut the door from the mudroom to the rest of the house and, stepping inside, put the kittens and the mama cat in the box of old towels.

Smokey eyed them suspiciously as her four kittens cuddled close, eyes still closed. "Keep an eye on 'em for me," he said.

He disappeared into the main part of the house, then came back with a small bowl of milk and a bowl of kibble. He set them down beside the washer and dryer, then walked over to the laundry sink and washed his hands. Susie followed suit.

He picked up his flashlight again. "So. Ready for our date?"

Susie squinted at him. "I thought the snipe hunt was our date."

"That," he said, taking her elbow and leading her out the door, "was only the preliminary."

Once again, Susie found herself briskly traversing the yard and tromping through the pasture grass. "So what are we looking for this time? Snakes?" she goaded, feeling warmth everywhere they touched, as well as where they didn't.

Tyler wrapped his arm around her waist, and with the other took her hand. Briefly, he two-stepped her around the pasture, before continuing on in the same matter-of-fact way toward some mysterious destination. "An oasis."

"Right. Of course."

Still moving, he cupped one of her hands in both of his. "You don't believe me, do you?"

She pivoted to face him. "I'm afraid not to believe you."

They walked in silence.

Susie tried not to think how good it felt, how right, to be there with him like this. Instead, she focused on how he had maneuvered events to his advantage, all the while keeping her in the dark.

"What if I'd said no to going out with you tonight?" she asked eventually, wishing she weren't thinking about taking Tyler in her arms again and claiming him as hers and hers alone. She didn't know how to deal with a relationship that had constantly expanding boundaries.

Tyler lifted her hand to his mouth and kissed the inside of her wrist. "You wouldn't have."

Susie's skin tingled at the brief, intimate contact. "How do you know?"

He wrapped his arm around her waist, and brought her closer yet, so their hips and thighs brushed as they walked. "Because you said yes."

Aware how easy it would be to fall in love with him and want so much more than either of them were prepared to give, Susie drew an unsteady breath. "Sure of yourself, aren't you?"

"Sure of you." He aimed a heart-stopping, sexy look her way.

Susie swallowed.

They came to another fence. Once again, Tyler gave her a boost up, one hand gripping hers, the other palming the back of her thigh and the underside of her bottom. His touch was practical, yet she felt the imprint of his touch long after he had pulled his hand away.

Once again, they started to cross a meadow beneath the starry Texas sky. And then, around a bend of mesquite trees, she saw it. An old-fashioned campfire, two canvas-backed camp chairs, a cooler and two glass lanterns.

He smiled at the stunned look on her face. "Welcome to dinner at Healing Meadow Ranch," he said.

"So I'm EXPECTED TO cook my own meal?" Susie watched as he started the campfire, built into the dirt, with the expertise of a man who knew his way around the great outdoors.

"An important factor in an interactive first date," he declared with a rakish smile.

Not just interactive, Susie thought. Memorable. As long as she lived, she would remember this night, and all the trouble he had gone to. "Good thing I love hot dogs barbecued on a stick, then."

He chuckled and handed her a long-handled fork, with a hot dog skewered on each prong. "I only brought a package of ten and eight buns, so pace yourself."

Good advice. If only she could adhere to it when it came to the inevitable good-night kiss at the end of the evening, Susie thought. Deciding it best to keep her mind out of the bedroom, she concentrated instead on the mundane. "Why do they do that? Package a different number of buns and weiners?"

Tyler regarded her with mock soberness. "It's an evil scam by the grocers. They want you to purchase four packages of hot dogs and five packages of buns so you'll come out even."

Susie shook her head and matched his droll tone. "Well, I'm alerted to it now."

"I would say you are." He handed her his fork to hold, and reached into the cooler.

To her astonishment, out came two large glass mugs, a carton of vanilla ice cream and two familiar brown bottles. He poured, scooped and stuck in a straw. "Root beer float anyone?"

They had to trade, his long-handled fork for her

drink. Susie batted her eyelashes at him in a parody of a pampered Texas belle. "Why, Tyler, you do spoil me," she declared.

His lively gaze lingered on her lips before returning, ever so slowly, to her eyes. "That's the general idea."

Basking in the carefree moment, Susie sipped with one hand, cooked with the other. "So, tell me, do you bring all your first dates out here?"

His smile turned tender, his glance direct. "You're the first," he told her softly.

Susie's heart did a little flip in her chest. She had secretly hoped this evening was as special to him as it felt to her. "Good to know," she said. She didn't know why she suddenly felt like bursting into happy tears, she just did.

Struggling to get her equilibrium back, Susie cleared her throat, sat back in her chair, and asked a great deal less sentimentally, "So what was your worst first date ever?"

Tyler exhaled. "My very first." He shook his head in disparagement. "I got a speeding ticket on the way to my date's house, which unfortunately I left on top of the car instrument panel and my date's father saw. He not only refused to let his daughter go out with me that evening, he called my dad."

Not fun. Susie made a face. "How old were you?"

"Sixteen. And it gets better. My parents had warned me about speeding but I had a lead foot and wasn't listening, so they grounded me and took away my truck keys, and it was another three months before I had another attempt."

Susie turned her fork, so the hot dog could cook on the other side. "What happened then?" she asked, sure from the look on Tyler's face that the rest of the story was even more entertaining.

"I hit another car when I was trying to parallel park at the movie theater."

Aware how cozy and intimate this all felt, she chuckled. "Yikes."

Tyler rolled his eyes in acknowledgment of his klutziness. "It wasn't even my pickup. I had borrowed my mother's very nice, very new SUV. I busted the other guy's taillight and dented my fender." He stretched his long legs out in front of him. "I don't really recall much about the evening because I was so terrified I had to go home and tell my folks what I had done, so I dropped my date off early. Ten-fifteen, I think. She never went out with me again."

Susie sipped some of her root beer float and found it every bit as delicious as it looked. "And I thought I had it bad."

Tyler turned his fork. "Your first date was bad, too?"

"Oh, yeah." Susie sighed, remembering. "I was sixteen, too. I'd had a crush on this guy from another high school forever. He finally asks me out. I finally convince my parents to let me go on an actual car date with a guy, alone, no chaperone, and I threw up in his car."

"Oh wow." Tyler looked stunned.

"Yeah." Susie turned quiet, reflecting. Surprising how she had forgotten this until now. "It was the first of a bad flu I couldn't seem to shake. Only of course it wasn't the flu. As we found out a month later, it was leukemia."

Tyler put his drink down and reached over and squeezed her knee.

Susie saw a wealth of compassion in his eyes.

"But it didn't end there," Susie said, determined to get the conversation away from the illness in her past, and back to a lighter tone. "Oh, no. Undeterred, I accepted another date the following week with someone from my own high school."

Tyler picked up his drink once again, and took a long draught. "The center on the basketball team."

"You remember that?"

Tyler shrugged. "He was a senior. So was I. Small town. Small school."

"Everybody knows everything about everybody else."

"Pretty much, yeah." He studied her. "So how did that date go?"

Susie tilted her head, curious. "You didn't hear?" She knew guys talked a lot in the locker room, and Tyler had been on the basketball team, too.

Tyler shook his head. "He was pretty close-mouth about it. You weren't talking, either, as I recall."

Susie flushed. "I was embarrassed."

Tyler's eyes narrowed in concern. "Why?"

Susie dragged the toe of her boot across the grass. She had gone this far, she might as well reveal the rest. "Because he drove us out to Lake Laramie to see the view, instead of where we were supposed to go that evening. He didn't want to take no for an answer, so he got one elbow in the chest, and a fist where it *really* hurts. And that was the end of that. He never spoke to me again, and I never spoke to him."

Tyler's jaw hardened. "Did you tell your parents?"

"Are you kidding? My mother and father would have killed him. Besides, I knew he'd never come near me again and he didn't and that suited me just fine."

Tyler scowled. "It's a good thing he lives in Alaska now. 'Cause if he were here, I'd have to hunt him down and settle an old score."

His irritated tone brought a smile to her lips. "You'd really do that for me?"

"Defend your honor? Without question," he said firmly.

The warmth was back, spiraling up inside her.

Making her want so many things. So many, in fact, she barely noticed the smoke spiraling up from the fire.

Tyler stopped holding her eyes long enough to nod in the direction of the campfire. "Darlin', I hate to tell you but I think your dinner's on fire."

Susie jumped up with an oath and blew out the flaming end.

"Good thing I brought a whole package," he drawled.

None of the rest of which either of them burned, although they did have a good time, talking and laughing and sharing confidences and stories about their youths that neither had heard before.

Not surprisingly, the evening was over all too soon.

Susie couldn't help but feel a little disappointed as Tyler put out the campfire, packed up the remains of their dinner and drove Susie home.

Every bit the gentleman, he came around to

open her door, then escorted her up onto the front porch of her house.

For once, Susie was very glad her residence was not visible from the street. At this moment, she longed for privacy.

Tyler stood in front of her, weight rolled forward on his toes, hands in the back pockets of his jeans. He mugged at her in comic seriousness. "I hope you're not expecting me to haul you against me and put the moves on you because I am not—I repeat not—the kind of person who kisses on the first date."

Susie couldn't help but laugh. "Well, lucky for you, cowboy, I am."

Chapter Nine

Live. Laugh. Love.

One kiss turned into two, then three, then four. By the time they reached five, they were inside the door.

"I thought we weren't going to rush things," he murmured.

Susie dropped her bag, every inch of her trembling with anticipation. She shrugged out of her coat. "Who agreed on that?" she teased, knowing what she'd thought she wanted wasn't what she yearned for at all.

"Life's short, Tyler," she continued, more seriously now, giving him a look that brooked no argument.

"Too short sometimes."

She helped him peel off his denim jacket, and went up on tiptoe. The tantalizing traces of his aftershave mingled with the clean scent of soap and the masculine fragrance of his skin.

Needing, wanting him as never before, she tangled her fingers in his hair and pulled him closer yet. "And we've waited too long."

His hazel eyes darkened and he flashed her a dangerous smile. "Way too long," Tyler agreed.

And then his lips were on hers, possessing her in a way she had always yearned for, making her heart pound, her senses swim and her feelings soar.

Susie moaned in surrender, allowing Tyler to consume her with his mouth. He used his lips, teeth and tongue until desire swept through her. Tenderness consumed her heart and the world narrowed to just the two of them.

He continued to hold and caress her, until all the layers of restraint fell away. She felt loved and protected, treasured in a way she had never been before.

Finally, he lifted his lips from hers and rested his forehead against hers while they both caught their breath.

"At this rate, I'm not sure we're going to make it to your bed," he whispered raggedly.

Merriment bubbled up inside her. She winked at him. "Then let's not." She captured his hand and led him only as far as her sofa. "I've always wanted to christen this."

He grinned, sinking down onto the couch, and

shifting her onto his lap. She felt the proof of his desire for her, saw the ardent light glittering in his eyes.

Thrilling tension and unbearable anticipation swept through her. And still he was content to take things slow, make every second last.

Which wasn't a bad idea, she thought, as she removed his shirt. He took off her sweater, and they resumed kissing again in a way that felt incredibly right.

Had she ever felt this happy or alive? Had she ever felt so womanly and sensual and free?

All Susie knew for sure was that being with Tyler this way, making love to him in the heat of the moment, was no longer enough.

She wanted more. Much more. She wanted a future that included him. She wanted to grow old with him. Do the impossible. Have a life...and a family...with him....

Tyler had planned a romantic evening for them. He had intended for them to have fun. He had wanted Susie to see at long last what he had realized, that the two of them had something special, something that would never be duplicated with anyone else. He wanted to show her that both of them still had a lot more loving and living to do. And he meant to do all that without taking her to bed.

But the moment she wrapped her arms around him and offered her lips up to his, all his gentlemanly instincts faded.

Need raced through him. Everything in him transmitted the strength of his yearning. Drunk with pleasure, he undressed her and found her soft curves.

She was incredibly beautiful. Her breasts nestled against the hard wall of his chest as his hands explored the silky smoothness of her inner thighs, the rounded curves of her buttocks.

He kissed her deeply, tasting the unique sweetness of her mouth. He flattened a hand over her spine and guided her even closer, reveling in her welcoming softness.

She rocked against him, leaving him with absolutely no doubt about what she wanted—what they both wanted now.

He set her aside, preparing to claim her as his.

Reclaiming control, she dropped her hands to his fly. "Let me help you with this," she murmured playfully, locking eyes with him.

He grinned, finding her passionate insistence as much a turn-on as the dampness between her thighs. "If you insist."

His jeans came down, shirt, shorts off.

She knelt between his legs, running her hands over the bunched muscles of his thighs, the flatness of his abdomen, the sensitive area beneath his sex.

He hardened even more. Worried it would be over all too soon, he cautioned, "Suze..."

"Let me," she whispered, lips and hands moving over him with utmost care. "Just...let...me..."

He let her call the shots, let her take him where she wanted him to go, until they were almost there.

Then his hands were on her shoulders, she was on her back, and he was stretched out over top of her.

She started to protest she wasn't finished loving him yet but the passion in his kiss soon had her surrendering to his will.

His gaze locked with hers, he pulled her legs to his waist, and slid between her thighs.

Her leg muscles tensed as he used his fingers to ease the way, and then they were together again, powerful sensations layered one over another.

He lay claim to her lips and body as he wanted to lay claim to her soul, giving her everything in return until she moaned softly.

Heart pounding, he slowed it down again, pausing, withdrawing and entering again, until she was kissing him back more passionately than ever before, arching her back and rocking up against him, clinging, holding, shaking with sensation.

And this time, when they came together in shattering sensation, he knew, there was no going back, not for either of them.

She belonged to him, and he to her. And that was the way it was always going to be.

THE NEXT MORNING, WHILE snuggling in the warm cradle of Tyler's arms, still trying to fully wake, Susie could not keep kidding herself.

She could soooo get used to this.

Like a fool, she'd told herself it would be enough to be friends.

Then lovers who were also dating.

Too late, she realized she had done the unthinkable.

She had fallen in love with Tyler McCabe. Not the kind of love you had for someone you'd known a long time, or relied on in times of need. The kind you had for a person you wanted to spend the rest of your life with, the kind you had for the person you wanted to marry.

Only they had agreed marriage wasn't in the cards for either of them. Tyler, because he either ran from or distanced himself in situations that were too tough to handle, emotionally. She, because of the possibility her leukemia might someday return and she didn't want to burden a spouse—or child—with having to see her through yet another potentially fatal illness.

And she'd thought she was all right with that.

She'd thought she was used to going it alone, with the family support system she had.

She'd thought she was okay, taking it one day at a time.

She hadn't thought she needed a man to love, or love her.

After last night, she knew differently.

Without Tyler in her life, she would never be this happy or feel this content. And yet, because she cared about him so much, she could not see herself saddling him with the fear she dealt with on a daily basis.

He was such a good man.

He deserved so much more than she could give him.

And she was just unselfish enough to want to see he had it.

"Okay, fess up," Tyler demanded, rolling onto his side. He propped his head on his elbow and gazed deep into her eyes. "What's on your mind now?"

Everything she had sworn she wouldn't even consider, she thought with wistful irony.

Susie rolled toward him. "I'm thinking about that Thanksgiving prep party we're supposed to attend at your parents' ranch this afternoon," she fibbed, not wanting anything to spoil the tenderness of this moment. Soon enough, they would have to talk about the limits she had imposed on herself. Limits that would now affect him, too.

Tyler stroked his fingers through her tousled curls, pressed a gentle kiss to her cheek. He seemed to know intuitively that she was holding back every bit as much as she was saying.

"What about it?" he asked her softly. He flattened a hand over the small of her back and guided her lower half against his.

A shiver of need swept through her.

She swallowed self-consciously and pressed her hands to his chest, shifting away from him. "One look at us and everyone's going to know—"

Half his mouth crooked up as he pulled her back into his arms. "That you love me?" he murmured sexily in her ear.

A flush started in the center of her chest, moved up into her neck, and face. "I didn't say that," she protested, embarrassed.

"You didn't have to." He shifted so she was beneath him and framed her face with his hands, his touch gentling even more. "It was in your kiss and the way you opened up to me, the way you snuggled against me all last night, the way you look at me when you think I don't see. The thing is," Tyler continued in a soft, straightforward voice that swiftly had her spirits soaring all the more. "I love you, too."

"YOU'RE REALLY GLOWING TODAY," Amy said.

Although Tyler and Susie had been busy since the moment they arrived at Annie and Travis McCabe's ranch, introducing Emmaline and her parents to everyone and helping the group of high school students put together the Thanksgiving gratitude journals—Susie felt as if she had a sign on her chest announcing Fool In Love. There was no doubt from the permanent smile on Tyler's face that he was gloriously content, too.

Amy walked with Susie across the Annie's Homemade product testing room where all the Thanksgiving-prep activity was going on, to the table where Amy had been preparing place cards. "What have you been up to?" Amy continued.

Susie sat down opposite her hopelessly romantic younger sister. Not sure how much she should tell, Susie shrugged. "Work. Lots and lots of work."

Amy handed Susie a list of names, a stack of cards and a calligraphy pen. "Uh-huh."

Susie surveyed the room until she found Tyler. He was laughing and roughhousing with his cousin, Brad McCabe's, preschoolers. It was hard to tell who looked happier, the children or Tyler.

Amy followed Susie's glance. "Tyler is really great with kids, isn't he?" Amy murmured.

Susie nodded. Funny, she had never really noticed how much Tyler enjoyed being around kids.

Until now. But there was no denying it, he was as good with teenagers like Emmaline, and his younger brothers Kurt and Kyle, as he was with the three- and four-year-old set....

Aware Amy was still observing her carefully, trying to figure out what was different, Susie smiled and went back to writing names on place cards. Deciding to shift the attention to their newly married sister, Susie asked, "Where's Rebecca? I thought she and Trevor were coming today."

"Rebecca's under the weather," Amy said, as Tyler and Teddy sauntered over to join them.

"Likely story," Teddy interjected with brotherly skepticism. He and Tyler sat down at the table with Susie and Amy. Seeming to have eyes only for his best friend in all the world, Teddy winked at Amy, and continued sagely, "I think they're home honeymooning."

Tyler shook his head, his expression suddenly one of concern. "I don't think so." In response to all the raised eyebrows, Tyler continued, "I saw Rebecca at the pharmacy yesterday afternoon. She looked a little green around the gills. She thought she was coming down with something."

It was the season for it, Susie thought.

"She was lamenting not having gotten a flu shot," Tyler continued.

"That explains where Rebecca is. But where's Trev?" Teddy said.

"Home taking care of Rebecca, like any good husband would," Amy explained.

Teddy grinned and planted both hands on his thighs. "I still say they're honeymooning. Have you seen those two lately? They're like a walking billboard for the advisability of marriage." He tilted his head to one side. "Should true happiness interest you, anyway."

Susie flushed as her emotions rose. "You don't have to be married to be happy," she disagreed, even though she thought that marriage was exactly what someone as family-oriented as Tyler needed to be truly blissful.

"Actually, I think you do," Annie McCabe interrupted, with a pointed look at her two single sons. She pointed at Tyler and Teddy with a merry twinkle in her eyes. "Which is why I'm on these two to find the women of their dreams and settle down, pronto."

Teddy groaned in a comic display of aggravation at the motherly advice.

Tyler, Susie couldn't help but note, merely looked thoughtful.

"WHY DIDN'T YOU TELL your mother how you feel about marriage this afternoon?" Susie asked later, when she and Tyler were on their way over to

Healing Meadow so he could check on Catastrophe and Smokey and the four kittens.

Tyler shrugged. "She knows how I've always felt. I've made no secret of that. Although," he said slowly with a telling glance at Susie, "I'm beginning to wonder if my attitude was a mistake. Just because I ran away from stuff that was hard to deal with emotionally when I was a kid doesn't mean I'd do it now with you. In fact," he said as his big hands gripped the steering wheel purposefully, "I'm certain I wouldn't."

Susie wished he didn't look so handsome in profile. She wished her body didn't react to his nearness. "What's changed?"

He gave her a look as if wondering that she even felt she had to ask. "Everything, in the last few days."

Susie looked out the window, at the scenery passing by. Desperate to move the conversation to safer ground, she said, "Emmaline sure seemed to hit it off with your cousins Kurt and Kyle, and Shane and Greta McCabe's four daughters."

Tyler nodded. "I think Emmaline's going to like being at Laramie Senior High School, once she's done with her chemo."

Susie thought so, too. She rubbed at the knee of her jeans with the flat of her palm, wondering if the subject of cancer would ever be less painful for her. Or if it would always carry with it the memory of the past and the fear of the future. "Emmaline's supposed to find out next week if she has to have any more treatments or if this last one was it."

"We'll hope for the best. In the meantime, you and I have the rest of the weekend to do whatever we'd like." Tyler planted a warm hand on her thigh and gave it an affectionate squeeze. "So, what's your preference?"

Glad to have the conversation back in territory she could deal with, Susie sent him a saucy smile. Already heating from his touch, she said, "Guess…"

To their mutual pleasure, the next five days passed quickly.

Tyler and Susie both had a lot of work to do, but they still managed to spend every night together, wrapped in each other's arms.

By the time Wednesday evening arrived, Tyler McCabe had become an essential part of her life. A fact, she knew, that was going to make it all the harder to let him go when the time came. Meanwhile, she intended to savor the present and enjoy every second they had together.

"I hope you're ready for this." Susie breezed into his kitchen, carrying two bags of ingredients she knew they would need.

A perplexed furrow formed between his brows. "I thought you were baking the pies."

Susie threw back her head and laughed, mentally chalking up the joy flowing through her to building holiday spirit. "You only wish." She batted her lashes at him flirtatiously. "We're doing it together while I teach you how to make them."

"Only one problem with that." Tyler set the three glass pie dishes onto the counter. "We didn't get any of those frozen crusts."

"We're going to make them from scratch."

Tyler looked apprehensive. He planted his hands on his waist and rocked forward. "Well, then I'm glad you know what you're doing," he drawled, just as playfully, "because I sure don't."

"Relax. It's really not that difficult."

"If you say so."

He watched Susie measure four and a half cups of flour into the bottom of a big mixing bowl, add two teaspoons of salt, and a cup and a half of shortening.

Savoring his nearness, she thrust a pastry blender into his large hand. Tightening her fingers over his, she showed him how to use it to cut the ingredients together.

While he mixed, she measured out ice water.

"You're right. This is kind of easy," he said, after a while.

Susie smiled.

Together, they added the water to the mixture until it formed a ball.

"Okay, now break that up into four equal pieces, and we'll be ready to roll the dough out," she explained, already sprinkling flour onto the wooden cutting board and rolling pin.

Tyler looked doubtfully at both.

"How about you do that while I peel the apples?" he suggested.

"Sure?"

"Positive. I'm a lot handier with a paring knife than a rolling pin."

"All you have to do is peel and quarter them. We can slice them in the food processor. It'll save time."

"I'm all for that." He gave her a sexy wink. "I don't want to spend all of this evening slaving over a hot stove."

Susie slapped the dough onto the cutting board. "Got a poetry reading in mind?"

"Something romantic," he affirmed.

Susie's heartbeat picked up. These days, it seemed they could not keep their hands off each other. Eyes still locked with his, she patted the dough flat with her hands. "Such as…"

"We'll have to finish this to find out," he declared with exaggerated seriousness.

"I'm sure we will," she countered drily, picking up the rolling pin.

"Then I plan to show you my…etchings."

Susie chuckled as she began to roll out the pastry. Tyler smiled, watching. Every inch of her felt vibrant, alive and healthy as all get-out.

Trying not to get used to this kind of hope-infused euphoria, she tore her eyes from his and looked past Tyler, into the laundry room. The door was open, the room quiet. Realizing what was amiss, she asked curiously, "Where are Smokey and her kittens?"

"One of the vet techs took 'em all home," Tyler said. "She's going to adopt Smokey and one of the kittens and find homes for the other three. It shouldn't be hard to do since Christmas is coming up."

Given how hard he had worked to find the missing felines, and how he had fussed over them since, Susie had thought—erroneously, she saw now—that he had developed a fondness for them that would spur him to keep at least some of them in his life. Instead, he had fallen back into old habits, doing what needed to be done to help an animal—or person—in need, and then moving on without a backward glance.

That should have been a comfort to her. Knowing he would bounce back when they inevitably had to part, and go their separate ways once again.

Instead, it left her feeling incredibly lonely and bereft.

Tyler set a peeled, quartered apple into the bowl Susie had provided. He paused, studying her face, obviously misunderstanding the reason for her concern. "I'm sorry. I didn't even think to ask. Did you want one of the kittens?"

Pets were a big responsibility, and a commitment of many, many years. In the past Susie hadn't had to think twice about whether or not to undertake something like that. With the exception of her business, which she had already arranged to leave to her sister Amy should anything happen to her, she had not pledged anything that would require time commitments that stretched into the future. For the first time, she was beginning to regret that attitude. And it was all because of Tyler. Because of all he made her long for now. All he still deserved.

Aware he was waiting for her answer, unwilling to spoil the mood with any talk about the future, she shook her head in reply. "I think I have my hands full, teaching you how to bake."

"No kidding." Tyler watched her fit one sheet of pastry into the dish, and pick up another pastry ball. He came closer, a studious look on his handsome face. "On second thought, maybe this is a skill I should learn. Mind if I try rolling out the dough?"

She smiled and stepped aside, her arm brushing his in the process. Aware she was tingling warmly from the small contact, she conceded graciously, "Not at all."

He took over with typical gusto, mimicking her actions right down to the sprinkling of flour over board, pin and dough. "This isn't as hard as I thought." He settled the flattened disc onto the center of the board, pushed the pin over the crust with masculine force, then frowned as the middle stuck to the pin and pulled all the way up, off the board. "On second thought, yes it is."

Susie stepped in and helped him disengage the pin and dough. "Just add a little more flour. Sprinkle it right there. And roll a little less forcefully." Susie put her hands over his and guided the rolling pin just so, moving it back and forth in a slow rhythm.

Tyler rocked with her, totally getting into the task.

"First time anyone's told me to do that," he teased.

Flushing at the unmistakable innuendo in his low tone, Susie replied with mock sternness, "Well, get used to it. Unless you're pounding out meat, a heavy touch is seldom required in the kitchen."

His brow lifted.

The heat inside her increased.

"What about the bedroom? What kind of touch is required there?"

"Oh, I think you've got the moves there down pat."

"Really?"

"Really."

He smiled, and kept rolling, back and forth, back and forth.

In and out, in and out.

Honestly, she had to stop thinking like that....

Had to stop wanting him like that.

Had to stop thinking that a life without him wouldn't be much of a life at all.

She'd been alone before.

She could—and would—be alone again.

Forcing her attention back to the task, she stepped away from him. Adapting the attitude of teacher, she observed as her "student" achieved the desired result, and clumsily transferred the flat disc to the glass pie pan. "See?" she praised, pleased and impressed. "You can do it."

Tyler turned and gave her one of his "Aw shucks, ma'am" grins. "I can do anything when I'm with you. You make me feel like a superhero." He inclined his head to one side in a parody of thoughtfulness.

She couldn't help but smile, he looked so darn cute, standing there with flour all over him.

Seeming to know just how attractive he was to her at that moment, he waggled his brows at her teasingly. "Or is it…Supercook?"

She rubbed at a smudge on his shirt. "We better stay focused or we'll never get this done."

He caught her hand and touched his lips to the inside of her wrist. Sensuality simmered between them, as potent and evocative as the fragrance of sugar and spice wafting up from the counters. "And we definitely want to get our work done so we can go play," he murmured, reeling her in for a long, heartfelt kiss.

Emotions in turmoil, she kissed him back. Then pushed at his chest. "Peel."

He sighed loudly and went back to the apples. "Slave driver."

"Yeah, well, you'll thank me later."

He waggled his eyebrows at her, giving an entirely new meaning to her words. "I imagine I will."

Fifteen minutes later, all the crusts were rolled out, the pumpkin pie was already in the oven, the pecan was ready to be put in, and Tyler was nearly done peeling the bag of crisp Granny Smith apples. Making short work of what could have been an arduous job, Susie ran them through the slicing blade of the food processor, then dumped them back into the bowl.

Tyler paused to taste a slice. He moaned appreciatively. "These apples are really good."

"They look good."

"Taste." He lifted one to her lips.

"Don't—" Susie started to say. Too late, he had popped apple in her mouth.

The flavor exploded on her tongue.

He laughed at the face she made.

"Wow, that's tart," she managed as soon as she finished chewing.

Grinning, he let his glance drift to the hollow of her throat, before returning to her lips, and then her eyes. Cupping her cheek with the flat of his palm, he ran his fingers through the hair at her temples. His eyes glimmered mischievously and his voice dropped another husky notch. "As long as you're puckered up…" He bent his head once again, and fit his lips over hers.

The sweet-tart flavor of apple mingled with the hotter, masculine taste of his mouth. Before Susie knew it, her arms were laced about his neck. They were kissing and kissing and kissing. Only the sound of the oven buzzer, signaling it was time to lower the temperature from 425 to 350, broke them apart.

"I knew you'd be a dangerous distraction in the kitchen," she joked, adjusting the temperature and bending to put the pecan pie in the oven alongside the pumpkin.

He traced the curve of her hips with both hands. "Not nearly as much of one as I'd like to be, believe me."

"Oh, I believe you, all right." Still tingling from his playful touch, she straightened, stepped away and reset the timer. The lust in his eyes was igniting her own. "Now, on to that apple pie filling..."

He made a face. "Taskmaster."

Someone had to be, if they didn't want to find themselves explaining how they'd come to either ruin or fail to complete three pies this evening. "When we're all done, two hours from now, you'll be thanking me for making such short work of this." And leaving the rest of their evening free for playing...

"I expect I will." Tyler took her into his arms again. Hazel eyes glimmering with affection, he bent his head. "But before we work anymore, I need another kiss."

Loving the way he made her feel, Susie was only too glad to oblige. They were still kissing when the doorbell rang.

"It seems to be our night to be interrupted by the bell," Tyler groused.

No kidding, Susie thought, as she reluctantly let him go. "You take care of that. I'll do this."

Grumbling his aggravation, Tyler disappeared.

Only to return a minute later, Susie's sister Rebecca, and his brother Trevor, by his side.

"What's up?" Susie asked the newly married couple.

It was clear from the color in their faces and the excitement in their eyes that something was going on.

"We have news," Trevor said, his voice hoarse.

Rebecca nodded. Her eyes were moist.

Her sister looked the way she had on her wedding day when she'd taken Trevor's hand at the altar and prepared to take their wedding vows. Susie put the clues together that until this point she had largely ignored.

They're still honeymooning...incredibly happy... Rebecca's under the weather....

And suddenly, she knew.

"You're pregnant, aren't you?"

Rebecca nodded. Tears of happiness spilled down her cheeks. "Oh, Suze. We're having a baby next June."

Tyler let out a whoop of pure delight and the

two brothers hugged and slapped each other on the back.

Joy flooded Susie's heart and she gathered Rebecca in her arms.

Susie didn't need anyone to tell her how happy and excited Tyler was. His joy for his brother was clear for all to see.

"Congratulations!" Tyler hugged Rebecca while Susie and Trevor embraced.

"This is great news!" Tyler continued, when everyone had pulled apart. "The folks must be ecstatic."

Rebecca dabbed at the happy tears running down her face. "That is an understatement," she said.

"If it weren't for the big Thanksgiving celebration tomorrow I think they'd already be knitting booties and planning the nursery," Trevor teased.

"Anyway, we'll let you get back to your baking. We have to go find Amy and Teddy. We want to tell them, too."

Susie and Tyler congratulated Rebecca and Trevor again as they walked them to the door. And then all fell silent as they returned to the kitchen.

"Wow," Tyler said eventually. Still looking a little shell-shocked, he rubbed his jaw. "I'm going to be an uncle."

Susie measured sugar, flour, cinnamon and salt

into a bowl. "Well, I guess this takes the pressure off the rest of us."

Tyler lifted a brow.

Susie poured the dry ingredients over the sliced apples and mixed it all thoroughly. "Your mom was talking last weekend, about how much she wanted you all married. Now that she's going to be a grandmother for the first time, I expect she'll be a little distracted."

Tyler rocked back on his heels. "I wouldn't count on that, at least not for long. My mom's serious about wanting to see us all settled down, with families of our own."

So was hers. Susie put the apples in the crust, and dotted the top with bits of butter. She paused to tilt her head and study him beneath lowered lashes. "Does it bother you, that you won't be making her happy that way?" she asked softly.

Tyler shrugged and slid his hands into the pockets of his jeans. "Who says we won't?"

Chapter Ten

If you try hard enough, you will succeed.

Tyler stepped closer, looking impossibly handsome and impossibly determined in the welcoming light of the kitchen. "Marry me."

Susie had known this was coming. She just hadn't expected the discussion to happen tonight. She swallowed, loving him so much, too much, really… "Tyler." She splayed her hands across his chest and hitched in a quick bolstering breath.

"I know," he murmured in a low, sexy voice that further stirred her senses. Ever so tenderly, he smoothed the hair from her face. "It's not something I should be asking you just yet." He kissed her lightly, persuasively and moved his torso in even closer, until his lower half rested against hers and she could feel the depth of his arousal. "I just want you to know where this is headed."

Susie did know and her fear of the future…

of letting him down…in any way…was breaking her heart.

He dropped kisses along the shell of her ear and buried his face in the curve of her neck. "I want you to know how much I care."

The next thing she knew he had an arm behind her back, another beneath her knees. One smooth move and she was swept off her feet and cradled against his chest. With long and resolute strides, he headed through the passageway that led to the master bedroom suite.

"Tyler." Susie drew in a quick excited breath. "We haven't finished baking."

"We will." Hazel eyes glittering playfully, he flicked the light switch with the back of his hand, then strode over to set her down next to the king-size bed. "But first things first."

Susie ignored the racing of her pulse and did her best to look as if she had little interest in making love with him again, when she knew darn well nothing could be further from the truth.

"If that were the case," she said, "you and I would still be putting together an apple pie."

Tyler grinned and gave her body a long, thorough once-over that promised untold delights. Slowly lifting his hot-blooded gaze back to hers, he said, "We'll get to that, I promise. In the meantime—"

he eased the sweater from her torso, the skirt from her hips "—I want you to let yourself go."

Her heart fluttered once in anticipation, then his lips covered hers in a kiss that was slow and sweet, urgent and commanding, soft and tempting. And Susie knew, no matter what the future held for them, she could not let the opportunity to make love with him once again pass her by. Standing on tiptoe, she wreathed her arms about his neck, and returned his kisses ardently, knowing no one had ever wanted her in such a fundamental way, knowing no one had ever made her want or hope for so much.

He peeled off her bra. Her panties went next.

She had just started on the buttons of his shirt when he went down on his knees in front of her. "Ladies first." Using the pads of his fingers, he traced the satiny petals, found and luxuriated in the dampness that flowed.

Susie swayed in his arms. They had barely started and already she could feel herself sliding inexorably toward the edge.

Tyler released a sound that was pure male triumph, using lips and hands, coaxing response after response from her, until she was trembling, aching to be filled.

She caught his head in her hands. "Now," she said.

He kissed the inside of her thigh. "We're getting

there. But you're right." He stripped off his clothes, lowered her to the bed, and lay down beside her. "It is time we got more comfortable."

He was hard as a rock as he stretched out over top of her and took her wrists in his hand, anchoring them above her head. Leaving no doubt about who was in charge, he kissed her long and deep and hard. The softness of her breasts molded to the hardness of his chest. Her senses swam with the scent and taste of him. She opened herself to him and Tyler claimed her with the unchecked abandon she had come to know and love. Susie wrapped her legs around him, reveling in the hot, insistent demand, the thrust and parry. She surged against him, welcoming the commanding male possession, the sizzling sensations sweeping through her. She took him deeper inside her, tightening her hold on him as slowly and deliberately as he was claiming her, knowing even as they reached the pinnacle that it wasn't going to last.

Tyler had known something was wrong, even before he and Susie started to make love. He had known, from the moment he suggested marriage, that Susie was not ready to be his wife or look that far into the future.

The hesitation in her soft golden-brown eyes was what had made him want to claim her, now, in the most emotional way possible. He knew it was the only way to make her face up to the fact that her need for him was every bit as deep and lasting as his need for her. And although that fact was undisputed, he could almost feel the sadness in her as they climaxed, and continued to kiss and hold each other, during the minutes that followed. It was almost as if she was saying goodbye to him.

Stunned, he pulled away from her and saw the tears sliding down her face.

TYLER'S HEART BEGAN TO beat like a bass drum.

These were not happy tears. Not even close.

These were the tears of a woman who was trying—however reluctantly—to say goodbye.

Reminded of all that was at stake here, Tyler tipped her chin to his and asked, "What's going on?"

Susie looked edgy and kissable, even as she became immediately defensive and elusive. "I don't want to talk about this tonight."

Her golden curls tousled from their lovemaking, Susie dressed and went back to the kitchen.

The rain that had threatened earlier had begun to fall in earnest now, adding to the dark, despairing feel the evening had suddenly taken on.

Tyler pulled on his clothes and followed her.

"It can wait until after the holiday," Susie said when he had joined her again.

Not in his opinion. Tyler positioned himself so

she had no choice but to look at him. "If something is hurting you, Suze, if I've done something wrong here, I want to know what it is."

With a dispirited sigh, Susie took the pumpkin and pecan pies out of the oven, set them on top of the stove to cool. She put the oven mitts aside and turned back to him, the unbearable sadness he had felt in their last kiss, on her face. "I can't marry you."

Tyler forced himself to show no reaction. He might not have wanted to hear this, but he had half expected her to say something similiar.

Still holding his eyes—even more reluctantly now, he noticed—she gulped. "I thought—I hoped—I could, but tonight when I saw you with Rebecca and Trevor, saw how joyful you were over their news…" Tears blurred her eyes. She shook her head and went back to assembling the apple pie. "I realized I could never do that to you."

Knowing touching her now would be a mistake, Tyler stood, arms crossed in front of him, watching her layer the top crust over the filling. "You could never do what to me?" he prodded eventually, when she did not go on.

Susie crimped the edges with more than necessary care. "Deprive you of a family of your own."

He waited until she had fluted the edges, cut slits in the top, reset the timer and slid the finished confection in to bake. He took her by the shoulders and held her in front of him.

She studied him, silently assessing and deciding, Tyler figured, if she should get any further involved with him. He wanted her to feel she could. He wanted her to feel, as he did, that together they could surmount any obstacle.

Assured of her attention, he said quietly, "I don't understand."

SUSIE KNEW HE DIDN'T.

That was what made this conversation so painful.

Finding his tender touch unbearably poignant now that her decision had been made, Susie shrugged off Tyler's light restraining grip. She forced herself to put aside her own selfish desires and remind, "The chemotherapy I took may have rendered me sterile, Tyler."

A fact, she noted silently, Tyler knew very well, as he had been around the day, years ago, when she had received the news.

"*May* being the operative word here, Suze." Tyler's expression remained implacable. "You don't know for sure you'll never be able to bear a child."

Susie stared at the toe of her boot. She wished like hell her intuition were telling her otherwise. "I know," she said stubbornly. Just as she knew, after seeing him happily interact with children of all ages, and delight over the news of his triplet brother's impending fatherhood, that a life without children would not be a fulfilling one for him.

"Fine, then." Tyler moved closer once again. He released a long, frustrated breath. "If that's the case—*and we don't know that it is*—we'll adopt."

Tears pushed behind her eyes. Susie blinked, refusing to let them fall, even as her heart filled with a mixture of bittersweet resignation and longing. "I can't do that to a child," she said in a low, strangled voice.

"Love them?" Tyler taunted. Irritation creased his handsome features.

Susie held up her arms to ward him off. "Start out being their mother when there is no guarantee I'll be able to finish the job."

Tyler jammed his hands on his waist. "You're in remission."

Now. Susie gritted her teeth and spelled it out for him. "I could just as easily go out of remission."

Tyler shook his head in exasperation. "Anyone, no matter how healthy, runs the chance of getting sick, Suze."

Frustrated he wasn't taking her or her concerns seriously, Susie angled her chin at him. "But my chances are so much higher, Tyler."

He stared at her a long, debilitating moment.

Susie felt as though she had not a single defense left. Still, she had to try to end this on a civil note.

"I know this isn't what you were expecting from me. It's not what I expected to happen, either." She swallowed around the growing knot of emotion in her throat. "But you'll be okay."

He closed in on her with a hurt in his eyes and a purposefulness that had her trembling. "You really think so."

Tears gathered in her eyes. "You helped me heal, Tyler. Just like you help every other wounded being that comes your way, whether animal or person. And I'll always be grateful to you for that." Her voice caught. She had to force herself to do the unselfish thing. "And now it's time for you to move on. Just the way you're doing with Catastrophe and Smokey and her litter of kittens."

Looking even more betrayed, he countered, "I'm able to let those animals go because it's part of my job. Because I can't possibly care for every homeless or neglected animal I make well."

"The point is, you can do it," she said evenly, studying the ruggedly handsome lines of his face. "You can heal and walk away. And that's what you need to do here, with me."

"That is not what this is about," he argued.

Susie's spirits sank even lower. "Then what is it

about?" she asked around the ache in her throat, and the stronger one in her heart.

Tyler continued staring at her, looking more grim and unhappy than she had ever seen him. "It's more than the fact you're afraid to commit to me, to marriage, to children." He paused, shook his head disparagingly, as if wondering why he hadn't seen it sooner. "You're afraid to love."

Susie merely wished that were the case.

The tears she'd been holding back began to fall. "I do love you." More than she had ever imagined that she could.

Angrily, she wiped her eyes. "Don't you see?" She put up her hands to keep him from taking her in his arms again, and deliberately backed away, her look warning him not to even try and touch her.

Her voice broke and pain spilled through both of them, as she concluded hoarsely, "That's why I have to let you go." So he would have everything he deserved. "Because I do love you so very much."

Tyler's face turned to granite. "If you loved me, you'd risk anything and everything to be with me," he scoffed in a low, censuring tone, looking at her as if she were a stranger he had no idea how to deal with. He stepped back, away from her, away from everything they had shared. "The fact you won't…speaks volumes."

AT NINE THE NEXT MORNING, the rain that had started the previous evening was coming down in torrents.

"Some Thanksgiving day," Tyler muttered, standing in his kitchen, cup of cold, untouched coffee in his hand.

The doorbell rang.

Hoping it was Susie, there because she'd come to her senses, he rushed to get the door.

No such luck. It was his mother.

"Oh, honey, I'm glad you're here." Oblivious to the disappointment raging deep inside him, Annie unfolded her umbrella and set it next to the door. She wiped her shoes on the welcome mat, then hurried inside. "We've had a change of plans. We can't have the dinner outside at our ranch. The testing center is too small."

Tyler had figured as much. He shut the door behind her. "I assume there's a bad weather plan?" he asked his mother.

Annie smiled. "Fortunately, yes. Beau Chamberlain has an empty soundstage we can use over at his movie studio. So we're rounding up all the tables and carting them out there. Which is where you and Susie come in." Annie paused, for the first time seeming to notice how dark and gloomy the interior of his house was. Eyes full of a mixture of motherly concern and curiosity, she rubbed her arms to ward off the chill of damp, November air and continued to study him. "We could really use both of you."

Figuring he might as well get the confessing over with, Tyler stated tersely, "Susie's not here."

A slight lift of auburn brow. "Oh?"

"I haven't seen her since last night," he admitted reluctantly.

"Oh."

Tyler exhaled. It wasn't his fault Susie had chickened out on loving him. He had offered Susie a future, marriage, children. She had turned it all down without a backward glance. "Don't look at me that way, Mom," Tyler warned.

Annie lifted her hands. "I can't help it. I had so hoped the two of you had finally come to your senses and seen what your father and I had noticed years ago."

Tyler shoved his hands through his hair. "And what is that?" he demanded.

"That the two of you are meant for each other."

Tyler strode into the kitchen, intent on getting a fresh, hot cup of coffee for both of them, only to find out the automatic shut-off feature on the coffeemaker had kicked in, leaving the brewed liquid every bit as stone-cold as the beverage in his mug. "Yeah, well, Susie doesn't believe that," Tyler muttered, dumping his cup in the sink.

Annie cast an approving look at the three pies on the kitchen countertop. She moved closer, her tone gentle. "The way Susie was looking at you last weekend, the amount of time she has been spending with you lately, says otherwise."

"I agree with you," Tyler said flatly. "Susie does not. She thinks she can't be with me because she had cancer and could conceivably get it at some time in the future again."

"You can't convince her we're all at risk for tragedy at some times in our lives?"

"I tried. Believe me," Tyler confessed, miserable all over again. He swallowed around the tightness in his throat. "I told her I'd take the risk. I even offered to adopt if it turns out she can't conceive because of the chemotherapy. But she's not changing her mind."

Another lift of the brow. "I see."

Tyler frowned at his mother. "You're looking at me like you think it's all my fault."

"Well—" Annie made an offhand gesture "—I know how you can be."

Tyler braced himself for the criticism sure to come. "And how's that?"

"Let's just say you can be rather abrupt in your decision-making process."

"So I'm quick to decide what is right and wrong in any given situation, so I'm quick to figure out what I want and go right after it? So what?"

"Let me remind you that it was only recently that you believed you weren't cut out for a lasting relationship of any kind, save those you already had with your own family."

No one had to tell him how shortsighted he had been, how foolishly hard on himself. "That's all changed, Mom."

Annie perched on the stool and looked at him compassionately. "When? How? Why?"

The answer to that was easy. Tyler's gut tightened at the memory. "It happened the day I heard Susie had taken her chemo wigs in to be worked on and I realized I could lose Susie all over again. The thought of that happening without me ever really having her in my life was unbearable to me."

"So you started pursuing her."

Tyler nodded. "And I stopped looking back, stopped worrying about things outside my control. The way things were going between us I thought—hoped—she had done the same."

"Now you realize that was not the case," Annie guessed, understanding in her low tone.

"Right." Tyler paced back and forth.

"And because Susie isn't just like you—because she didn't make up her mind in the heat of the instant and stick with it—you're dropping her like a hot potato," Annie concluded tartly.

Tyler winced and swung back around. "I didn't break up with Susie, Mom. She broke up with me."

"Mmm-hmm." Annie remained unimpressed. "And you're accepting it."

Tyler heard a wealth of accusation in that single sentence. He clenched his jaw. "I assume there is a point here?"

His mother smiled. "Since when do you give up on anything you want?"

"I THOUGHT I MIGHT FIND you alone this morning," Meg Carrigan said, shaking off the rain before stepping inside the potting shed behind Susie's business.

Susie put up a gloved hand. She was wearing jeans and an old sweatshirt. She had to leave in an hour, and she still hadn't showered. Meg, on the other hand, looked ready to go.

"I already heard about the change of venue for the dinner," Susie said.

Silence rebounded between them. Meg stepped closer, being careful not to brush up against the dirt-smeared wooden table. She did not look at all surprised to find Susie working on a holiday, even though the landscape and garden center was closed. Maybe because Susie had done it so many times before.

"That's not why I'm here," Meg said quietly.

Susie took a deep breath and then through sheer force of will, pushed back the tears she could feel gathering behind her eyes. The scent of leafy plants, damp air, and fresh dirt lent an earthy smell to the shed she found a lot more comforting than her thoughts, most of which centered around Tyler McCabe, and the love and passion they had found, and then been forced—for his sake—to give up.

Susie swallowed around the tightness of her throat. "Then why are you here?" she asked eventually.

Meg fingered the yellow blossom and red leaf on a holiday poinsettia plant—one of many Susie was preparing for sale. "I figured you might be upset about Rebecca and Trevor's news."

"I'm happy for them, Mom." Susie set one gold-foil-wrapped pot aside, picked up another.

"Of course you are." Meg continued to study Susie, as usual, not missing a trick. "You're also sad for you."

Susie refused to look at Meg as she concentrated on her work. "I dealt with the ramifications of my chemo long ago," she reminded her mother numbly.

Meg gently shook her head. "If that were true,

you would have been out having tons of fun and dating all these years instead of slaving away like there was no tomorrow."

Susie kept her head down. "I was building a business."

"And hiding from the possibility of more pain. I know," Meg said with compassion, laying her hand on Susie's arm, "because I've done it, too."

Susie looked up, aware her heart was pounding. "When?"

"During the years before your father and I married."

Feeling more hopeless and depressed than ever, Susie picked up another decorative plastic container and partially filled it with planting soil. "I don't see the comparison."

"Don't you?" Meg challenged. "I waited five years before telling him I had become pregnant and given birth to his child."

"Your reasons were noble," Susie argued back, tamping the soil down around the plant. "You knew my dad had already married someone else and started a family of his own. You didn't want to disrupt that."

Meg nodded sagely. "That's what I told myself." She paused to make sure Susie was listening. "The *reality* was I deprived Luke of the first five years of Jeremy's life. Had your father and I not serendipitously ended up taking jobs in the same place, we might never have seen each other again, I might never have known your mother had died, and Luke was struggling to bring you three girls up on his own the same way I was struggling to rear Jeremy on my own."

"What does that have to do with my situation?"

"I just talked to Annie McCabe. Trevor told her you broke up with him last night."

Susie hadn't known she could hurt this much. She hadn't known she could love this much. "It's for his own good. I would never have even gotten involved with him if it hadn't been for the fact that he always said he didn't want to marry or have kids. I took him at his word," Susie remembered wistfully. "Then I saw him with all the kids on Saturday." Her tears started once again. "I saw the joy in his eyes when he learned Trevor and Rebecca were expecting a baby." Susie paused to remove her glove and wipe her eyes. "I knew it would be wrong to deny him that."

Meg rummaged in her pocket for a tissue. "And he just accepted your excuse."

"No." Susie blew her nose. "He argued with me. Said we could adopt."

Meg looked more thoughtful than upset. "But you don't want to do that."

Susie released a quavering breath, shook her head. "I don't want to hurt him, Mom."

Meg reached over and patted her hand. "It's a good thing you're not doing that now, then."

Chapter Eleven

Never give up. Never ever ever give up.

The rain had stopped by the time Susie arrived at the Chamberlain Movie Studio, just outside of Laramie, Texas, at noon on Thursday. The sky was still gloomy, the ground still glistening with dampness, but the air that had been so cold and wintry the night before was warming up. By the time they sat down to dinner at five, it might actually be sunny.

At least Susie hoped that would be the case, as she lifted the large box of Thanksgiving gratitude journals from the front seat and headed inside, where tons of activity was going on. Tables were being set up, cloths smoothed, centerpieces unpacked, a temporary kitchen set up.

Fortunately, the table designated for the gratitude journals was easy to find. Susie'd just set her box down next to it when Emmaline Clark came skipping up to her. Emmaline was wearing one of

Susie's old wigs. It had been cut and adjusted to fit her pixie face. Despite her thinness, Emmaline looked happy as could be. "Guess what?" Emmaline announced, beaming. "I've had my last chemotherapy treatment!"

Susie enfolded her in a hug. "Oh, honey, that's wonderful!"

Emmaline hugged Susie back, then helped her stack journals onto the tabletop, chattering all the while. "I get to go back to school as soon as I get my strength and weight up. And in the meantime, I've got plenty of company. Kurt and Kyle and their cousins have all been stopping by to see me."

"They're great kids."

Emmaline looked in the direction from which she'd come. A group of high school kids were motioning for Emmaline to join them.

"Well, I've got to go." Emmaline and Susie stacked the last of the journals side by side. "I just wanted to tell you my news. And let you know I haven't forgotten my promise to work for you at the landscape center next spring."

Susie nodded. "I'll be looking forward to it."

Emmaline dashed off. Susie picked up the empty box. A familiar set of footsteps sounded behind her. She turned, expecting to see Tyler and found his brother, Teddy, standing there instead.

Her face fell.

"Don't look so happy to see me," Teddy teased.

Susie flushed. "Sorry."

Teddy relieved her of the empty box. "I'll take care of this. You're needed on Soundstage 16."

Susie paused. "Why?"

Teddy shrugged in that amiable way of his and lifted his hands. "I don't know. I don't ask questions. I just follow orders." He winked. "And I'd advise you to do the same."

Susie knew the last-minute change of venue had created a lot more work for everyone. Although the women in charge seemed to be handling it well. Susie wished she were as calm. That was a tall order, given the mess her personal life was currently in.

Susie studied the laid-back horse rancher who was also her sister Amy's best friend in the world. And like every other McCabe man, a real stand-up guy.

Susie swallowed around the tightness of her throat. "Have you seen Tyler?"

"Here?" Teddy scanned the large soundstage, which was being set up like a fancy ballroom, complete with velvety red-and-gold carpeting and a raised parquet dance floor. "Not yet."

"Okay." Disappointed, Susie started to move away. Then stopped, turned back, not caring how it looked, she had to know. "But he is coming today, isn't he?" she asked anxiously.

"So far as I know. Why?" Teddy looked curious. "Is there some reason Tyler wouldn't show up?"

Susie did not want to go there.

She shrugged and smiled. "I better get a move on."

To her relief, Teddy made no attempt to stop her. Susie headed out of the big brick building to the parking lot. Guests were still arriving in droves. Susie scanned the area but she did not see Tyler's pickup truck as she made her way through the sea of buildings, noting the bold black numbers painted on the side of each, until she found Soundstage 16.

She walked to the door, stepped inside.

Wondered promptly if she had made a mistake.

The soundstage was set up as an old-fashioned saloon, suitable for the Old West. That was not surprising, since Beau Chamberlain's movie studio primarily filmed movies with Western settings.

What was unusual was that there was no one else around.

Nothing she could see that needed to be carted back to the Thanksgiving festivities.

And that was when the swinging doors behind her opened, and a cowboy handsome enough to star in a film walked through.

TYLER HAD KNOWN IT WAS a risk, setting Susie up this way, but he wanted their conversation to be private. Fortunately, family friend Beau Chamberlain had understood and given him the keys to this building.

Susie caught her breath at the sight of him. He felt like doing the same. She was a vision, blond curls a golden halo about her head, cheeks flushed pink, golden-brown eyes shimmering with unchecked emotion. She was wearing one of those long flowing skirts she favored. Today's was a beautiful burgundy. A matching V-neck sweater with three-quarter sleeves hugged her slender torso, emphasizing her delicate curves. A cameo necklace on a strand of velvet adorned her neck, dangling orbs hung from her ears.

She came closer.

He noted she had on her fancy suede high-heeled boots instead of her usual sturdy engineer's boots. And she smelled every bit as heavenly as she looked, he noted, closing the distance between them.

Like a meadow of flowers after a rain.

When the two of them were close enough to touch, they squared off. She tipped her face up to his. "What's going on?" she asked in a soft, serious voice.

Tyler wanted her comfortable before they began

what might be the most important and possibly difficult conversation he'd ever had in his life. He nodded at the fully functioning movie set behind them. "Want a drink?"

Susie twined her hands together. Her eyes remained on his. "I'd prefer an explanation." Abruptly, she looked as nervous and out of sorts as he.

Tyler nodded, aware she had every right to be on edge, given the way things had ended between them the evening before. "Take a seat at the bar," he told her huskily, "and I'll try to give you one."

Susie walked over, her long full skirt swirling over the top of her calf-high boots. She climbed up on a stool and rested an arm on the top of the polished mahogany bar.

Tyler moved behind the counter, and got out two tall tulip-shaped glasses. He winked at her. "One sarsaparilla coming up."

She grinned at his choice of beverage.

He hoped this was a good sign.

Tyler filled the glasses with the nonalcoholic carbonated drink popular in the Old West. "I know I'm an old-fashioned guy." Tyler slid the glasses across the bar and came around to join her.

He nixed the seat and stood beside her, facing her, one elbow on the bar. Telling himself the cool reservation in her eyes was only to be expected, he continued softly, "The thing is, Suze, I think you are just as traditional at heart." Tyler covered her hand with his own, tightened his fingers over hers. "Which is why I proposed marriage in the first place. I figured if you and I were going to be spending every night together we might as well go ahead and make it a lasting arrangement."

Okay, Susie thought, studying his hazel eyes. This wasn't quite what she was expecting to hear, any more than his superpragmatic attitude was what she had hoped to witness.

But still…a step in the right direction, however small…could only be appreciated for what it was.

A step closer to their goal.

Tyler rubbed his thumb across the inside of her wrist. "I assumed—wrongly, I see now—that we were on the same page."

The regret in his tone had her nerves jumping. Beginning to see she had done her job being noble far too well, she told him, "We were."

Tyler shook his head and his mouth twisted in a rueful line. "That was presumptuous of me. And if there is anything a true gentleman should never be, it's presumptuous when it comes to his lady."

His lady.

Susie paused, knowing pride was an easy thing to let go of, considering all that was at stake. Gathering her courage around her like an invisible cloak, she put her hands across the warm solid wall of Tyler's chest, and whispered, "I thought we broke up." *Were still broken up...*

"That's the thing about us ranchers." He began to grin his sexy mischief and lust smile that she loved so much. "We're pretty good at fixing things."

"I see," Susie murmured, spirits lifting even as she studied him in fascination. She could see the desire in his eyes and the shiver inside her intensified. "And how do you intend to fix this?"

Tyler lifted her hand to his lips and kissed it gently, like a knight paying homage to his queen. "By giving you whatever you need, whenever you need it." He drew her to her feet, and into his arms. "If that's space, then you've got it." He sifted a hand through her hair. "If it's companionship or sex or just a friend to talk with then you've got it. And if it's love," he murmured, tilting her face up to his, "you will always have that. Because I love you, Susie, with all my heart. So whatever terms you want to set out for us," he told her gruffly, "are going to be just fine."

"Oh, Tyler." Susie flushed with heat from head to toe, aware she had never been happier. She closed her eyes as his lips moved over hers, once and then again and again in a sweet, lasting kiss that spoke volumes about what they felt. Yet there was still so much she needed to say to him, too. Slowly, reluctantly, she pushed him away and ended the kiss.

"I can't ask you to do all the giving when you're getting nothing in return," she told him, ready now to make the changes she had been afraid to make before.

Tyler's eyes darkened seriously and his low voice filled with all the love and tenderness he felt for her. "All I need is you, Susie."

She shook her head, knowing that love required equal sacrifice and commitment from each partner. Otherwise it would never work. "Hear me out," she said in a rusty-sounding voice.

His arms tightened around her. "I'm listening."

Susie drew another even more tremulous breath. "You were right about me." She swallowed. "I am scared. I'm always going to be scared. That doesn't mean I have to let my anxiety rule our lives. I want to be with you. I want to keep taking risks, and putting my heart on the line. I want to have a family, and I want to have it with you, because I love you, too, with all my heart and soul."

He grinned, ecstatic, and touched his lips to hers. "We are on the same page."

Susie wrapped her arms around his neck and went up on tiptoe. She touched her lips to his. "And always will be."

They shared another kiss, deeper, more lasting.

"So, does this mean you'll marry me?" Tyler prodded at long last, the way he was holding her leaving no doubt about the depth of his commitment to her.

Her heart overflowing with love, Susie kissed him back, until she was sure he knew how much she adored him, too, until they both felt the promise of the future, and the complete joy of the present. "As soon as I can."

They hugged each other fiercely. "Let's go tell everyone our news," Tyler said.

Hand in hand, Susie and Tyler walked back to the soundstage where everyone had gathered. All their family, everyone they loved, was present. The banquet area was a festive scene, bustling with activity. The tantalizing aroma of roast turkey and cornbread stuffing filled the air. Buffet tables brimmed with an array of lovingly prepared side dishes and desserts.

Looking like he had just won the lottery, Tyler stepped to the center of the room and quickly got everyone's attention. "Guess who just agreed to make me the happiest man on earth?" he announced.

A cheer went up among the guests. Congratulations and a bounty of good wishes followed.

"This is going to be a Thanksgiving we'll always remember," Susie's parents said happily, hugging them both.

At long last, Susie noted, Meg and Luke thought Susie had it all.

"We heartily concur!" Annie and Travis McCabe said together, both of them grinning.

"We really are blessed," Susie told Tyler, her voice catching slightly and her eyes brimming with happy tears, as they made their way to their seats.

Tyler wrapped his arms around her and held her close, all the love he felt for her in his touch. "The gratitude we feel today is just the beginning, Suze," he told her tenderly. "We have so much to look forward to."

So much indeed.

Smiling, Susie and Tyler took their seats among family and friends. They linked hands and bowed their heads as grace was said.

* * * * *

YES! Please send me the *Cowboy at Heart* collection in Larger Print. This collection begins with 3 FREE books and 2 FREE gifts in the first shipment, and more free gifts will follow! My books will arrive in 8 monthly shipments until I have the entire 51-book *Cowboy at Heart* collection. I will receive 2 or 3 FREE books in each shipment and I will pay just $4.99 U.S./ $5.89 CDN. for each of the other four books in each shipment, plus $2.99 for shipping and handling.* If I decide to keep the entire collection, I'll have paid for only 32 books because 19 books are FREE! I understand that by accepting the 3 free books and gifts places me under no obligation to buy anything. I can always return a shipment and cancel at any time. My free books and gifts are mine to keep no matter what I decide.

256 HCN 0779   456 HCN 0779

Name	(PLEASE PRINT)	
Address		Apt. #
City	State/Prov.	Zip/Postal Code

Signature (if under 18, a parent or guardian must sign)

Mail to the **Harlequin® Reader Service:**
IN U.S.A.: P.O. Box 1867, Buffalo, NY 14240-1867
IN CANADA: P.O. Box 609, Fort Erie, Ontario L2A 5X3

* Terms and prices subject to change without notice. Prices do not include applicable taxes. Sales tax applicable in N.Y. Canadian residents will be charged applicable taxes. This offer is limited to one order per household. All orders subject to approval. Credit or debit balances in a customer's account(s) may be offset by any other outstanding balance owed by or to the customer. Please allow 4 to 6 weeks for delivery. Offer available while quantities last. Offer not available to Quebec residents.

REQUEST YOUR FREE BOOKS!
2 FREE NOVELS PLUS 2 FREE GIFTS!

HARLEQUIN®

American ★ Romance®

LOVE, HOME & HAPPINESS

YES! Please send me 2 FREE Harlequin® American Romance® novels and my 2 FREE gifts (gifts are worth about $10). After receiving them, if I don't wish to receive any more books, I can return the shipping statement marked "cancel." If I don't cancel, I will receive 4 brand-new novels every month and be billed just $4.49 per book in the U.S. or $5.24 per book in Canada. That's a savings of at least 14% off the cover price! It's quite a bargain! Shipping and handling is just 50¢ per book in the U.S. and 75¢ per book in Canada.* I understand that accepting the 2 free books and gifts places me under no obligation to buy anything. I can always return a shipment and cancel at any time. Even if I never buy another book, the two free books and gifts are mine to keep forever.

154/354 HDN FV47

Name	(PLEASE PRINT)

Address	Apt. #

City	State/Prov.	Zip/Postal Code

Signature (if under 18, a parent or guardian must sign)

Mail to the **Harlequin® Reader Service:**
IN U.S.A.: P.O. Box 1867, Buffalo, NY 14240-1867
IN CANADA: P.O. Box 609, Fort Erie, Ontario L2A 5X3

Want to try two free books from another line?
Call 1-800-873-8635 or visit www.ReaderService.com.

* Terms and prices subject to change without notice. Prices do not include applicable taxes. Sales tax applicable in N.Y. Canadian residents will be charged applicable taxes. Offer not valid in Quebec. This offer is limited to one order per household. Not valid for current subscribers to Harlequin American Romance books. All orders subject to credit approval. Credit or debit balances in a customer's account(s) may be offset by any other outstanding balance owed by or to the customer. Please allow 4 to 6 weeks for delivery. Offer available while quantities last.

Your Privacy—The Harlequin® Reader Service is committed to protecting your privacy. Our Privacy Policy is available online at www.ReaderService.com or upon request from the Harlequin Reader Service.

We make a portion of our mailing list available to reputable third parties that offer products we believe may interest you. If you prefer that we not exchange your name with third parties, or if you wish to clarify or modify your communication preferences, please visit us at www.ReaderService.com/consumerschoice or write to us at Harlequin Reader Service Preference Service, P.O. Box 9062, Buffalo, NY 14269. Include your complete name and address.

HARDIR13

ReaderService.com

Manage your account online!

- Review your order history
- Manage your payments
- Update your address

> **We've designed
> the Harlequin® Reader Service
> website just for you.**

Enjoy all the features!

- Reader excerpts from any series
- Respond to mailings and
  special monthly offers
- Discover new series available to you
- Browse the Bonus Bucks catalog
- Share your feedback

Visit us at:
ReaderService.com